Presented by
Colorado School and Public Employees
Retirement Association
May 2011

copyright © 2008 Michelle M. Barone
illustrations © 2008 Tara McMillen

book layout design by Phat Vuong
phatvuong.com

PURPLE SKY PUBLISHING
PO Box 12013, Parkville, MO 64152
www.purpleskypublishing.com

LCCN 2007937177
SAN 256-5994

Publisher's Cataloging-In-Publication Data
(Prepared by The Donohue Group, Inc.)

Barone, Michelle M.
    The Capitol ghost mystery / written by Michelle M. Barone ; illustrations by
Tara McMillen.

    p. : ill. ; cm.

    Summary: A young girl attempts to unravel a series of puzzling happenings at
the Denver, CO Capitol building.
    ISBN: 9780976901778

1. Colorado State Capitol (Denver, Colo.)--History--Juvenile fiction. 2.
Ghosts--Colorado--Denver--Juvenile fiction.   3. Denver (Colo.)--Juvenile
fiction.   4. Colorado--History--Juvenile fiction.   5. Colorado--Capital and
capitol--History--Fiction.   6. Ghosts--Colorado--Denver--Fiction.   7. Denver
(Colo.)--Fiction.   8. Colorado--History--Fiction.   9. Mystery and detective
stories. I. McMillen, Tara. II. Title.

PZ7.B37 Ca 2008
[Fic]   2007937177

Printed in Canada

~ • ~

For my daughter Alexandra
and my nieces Natalie and Jacqueline.

~•~

Acknowledgements:

I thank Stephen J. Brooks for his vision of creating a magical world for children through books and for his input on this one. I thank my first readers: Cynthia Camp, Alex Barone-Camp, Paula Bennett, Sheryl Connet, Marcia Hoehne, Claudia Brett-Goldin, ELI Goldin, and Sophie Goldin. I thank Edna Pelzmann and Simon Maghakyan from the Colorado State Capitol. And I thank everyone of you for reading the Capitol Ghost Mystery.

Chapter 1

Things happen. Sometimes they are coincidental. Sometimes they make no sense. And sometimes they seem meant to be. They fall into place perfectly.

The Dora Moore School's traditional fifth-grade trip to the Colorado State Capitol was almost canceled. The portrait of Abraham Lincoln had been stolen from the third floor Presidents' Gallery the day before. It was the Capitol's second portrait of Lincoln and the second one to be stolen. The first one vanished in October of 1994. There were rumors that the historic Capitol was home to a number of ghosts, but this was a human crime.

Silvie Blake heard all about it on the morning news while she and Gramps ate breakfast.

"The painting of Lincoln disappeared in broad daylight," said the T.V. newscaster. "Nothing else is missing except two 'Wet Floor' signs."

"Who would do such a thing? Surely that painting isn't worth much money," Gramps said. "The world is full of kooks! They must be crazy!"

"Yeah," agreed Silvie. "Why would somebody take Lincoln and none of the other presidents' portraits?"

"The Capitol will remain closed to the public," the newscaster went on, "however, prearranged field trips for school children will be held as scheduled."

Silvie got up from the table and did a few ballet twirls through the main level of the Denver Square styled house. She stopped in first position to bend down and kiss Gramps. Silvie rubbed her tabby cat Millie's ears. She grabbed her backpack, stuffed her sack lunch inside, and headed for the door.

On her way out she glanced at the portrait of Mama hanging in the entryway. It had been crudely painted by her father over a decade ago. He drifted into and out of Mama's life long enough to leave her this amateurish portrait and a baby. The painting was a constant reminder of the parents who had both faded from Silvie's world. But for the moment, Silvie was more interested in the Capitol's stolen painting of Lincoln than the portrait staring back at her.

Silvie walked out the front door and turned her thoughts to the field trip ahead. She had to get through only one more day at school and then she would be free for a whole week during spring break; free from Ms. Crabtree asking her to speak up in class, free from kids staring at her and whispering, free from being alone in the middle of fifth grade.

A field trip to the Capitol would help the last day before spring break pass more quickly. Besides, Silvie liked solving puzzles. She was good at it. Today she would get a look at the scene of the crime.

Chapter 2

A mile away Dwayne Beasley read the morning headlines through the glass window on a newspaper machine outside Smiley's Laundromat. He didn't have a quarter to buy a paper. If he had the money he wouldn't spend it on a newspaper anyway. Yes indeed, the painting of Abraham Lincoln was stolen yesterday, but the effort had been worthless. That's what Beasley got for listening to the ranting of a homeless woman. She didn't drink the money she begged for like the rest of the wanderers living under the viaduct at Speer Boulevard. Since she wasn't an alcoholic, Dwayne Beasley had thought her story of the State Capitol, a riddle about Lincoln, and a fortune were true; but he was wrong.

Once Dwayne got inside the capitol he found the portrait of President Lincoln easily enough. He stole it easily enough, too; but he found no riddle and no treasure. At least the painting made the campsite look more homey afterward for everyone who lived outside, including Dwayne. Before he left this morning he wrapped the portrait in an old blanket.

Traffic was picking up on Colfax. Thursdays were usually good begging days, and Beasley wanted to be the first one to claim the corner of Colfax and Josephine. Dwayne turned away from the newspaper machine and started walking east.

Thirty minutes later, Silvie Blake waited for the light to change before she crossed the street. She knew that with four lanes of traffic on Colfax it was too risky to walk across without the green light in her favor. It was risky even with the green signal. Other kids joined her on the corner to wait for the light. Silvie pulled her dark hair forward to cover the marks on her cheeks. If only she hadn't yanked that bowl of hot potato soup onto herself when she was three years old. Now because of one wrong move as a toddler, she was scarred for life.

"Green light!" yelled a fourth-grade boy in Silvie's ear.

The mob of school children walked across the street, heading for the corner where a heavily whiskered man holding a cardboard sign begged for spare change.

"Anything helps," was scrawled on the sign.

"Hi kids," said the homeless man.

Something moved in Silvie's heart. She reached into her pocket, and handed the man a nickel and four dimes.

"Thanks," he said. "My name is Dwayne, what's yours?"

Silvie smiled, but said nothing. She walked behind the group of kids keeping close enough to look like she was part of them. She had lived in the city all of her life, and Mama had taught her well. Silvie knew how to keep safe around strangers.

"You look familiar. I think I know you," called Dwayne.

Silvie kept walking.

Chapter 3

Silvie did not look back at the scruffy man. I'm not taking any chances, she thought, sticking close to the other kids. Ten minutes and eight blocks later she could see the castle-like peaks of the ornate, three-story, red-brick school. Dora Moore Elementary was on the Denver Historical Society's list as a structure to be preserved for eternity. Mama and Gram had gone to this same school.

It's strange how buildings exist through many human lifetimes, she thought. It's as if they silently watch time and generations pass by. But she ended the thought there. Silvie wasn't very interested in history. It was all she could do to handle the present.

The bell was ringing as Silvie crossed the playground. She arrived at the perfect time, not early enough to play with friends she didn't have, and still in time for the start of school. After the opening routine and a spelling test, Ms. Crabtree's class gathered sack lunches, jackets, notebooks and pens for the field trip.

"Let's get outside. A bus will be here soon to take us to the Capitol," said the teacher.

Silvie's classmates pushed and shoved themselves into a jagged line. Gramps was right. The world was full of kooks. Silvie felt like she was looking at a bunch of them right now.

Outside the school, Silvie clutched her notebook as she waited in line. She knew that every minute the bus was late there was a greater chance for kids to misbehave, for mischief to start, for things to go wrong.

Without warning, two boys smashed her from behind. Silvie fell into the girl standing in front of her.

"I'm sorry, Maggie," Silvie mumbled recovering her balance.

"Adam Samuel Westin the Sixth! Stop pushing!" ordered Ms. Crabtree. "Are you okay, Silvie?"

Silvie nodded.

"Speak up, Silvie!" said Ms. Crabtree.

"Yes Ms. Crabtree, I'm fine," Silvie replied, loudly.

Adam Westin was still on the ground staring up at her. Silvie pulled her hair forward over her cheeks wrapping it closer around her face like a mother tucking a baby in a blanket.

"Leave Silvie alone, you bullies," said Maggie.

"Waffle-face is fine," said Adam, getting up.

Silvie stared straight ahead. She'd heard it all before. Ever since she started school kids had teased her, or pointed, or stared. It was easier when she could go home and talk with Mama. Her mother always said something that took away the sting. That was before Iraq and the war, and before Mama didn't come home.

"You'd better be careful Silvie, or you'll scare the ghosts at the Capitol today," said Adam.

"What are you talking about?" demanded Maggie.

"The Capitol's haunted. My dad knows. His law office is a block away. He hears stories about the Capitol all the time. It's full of ghosts, real ones, only I bet we won't see any today because Silvie's face will scare them away!"

Adam Westin is a definite kook, thought Silvie.

"We won't see any ghosts because there aren't any!" said Maggie.

"The ghosts are there, and I bet they know who stole the Lincoln painting," said Adam.

"I think a regular person is going to have to solve that crime, Adam," said Silvie. She didn't mean to join the conversation, but she couldn't help herself. "You probably think the school's haunted too."

"It's old enough to be haunted. Look! There's a ghost in the window," said Adam, pointing.

Silvie turned to look with everyone else.

"Oops, it disappeared. Silvie's face scared it away," said Adam.

"You're being cold-blooded now, Adam," said Josh, another boy standing close by.

"There's no such thing as ghosts!" said Maggie. "Silvie, tell them how sticks and stones may break your bones but words can never hurt you."

Silvie winced. Whoever made up that silly saying didn't have something wrong with them like a deformity or a defect, or an obvious difference that kids could pick at over and over like a scab on a wound that wouldn't heal.

"It's nothing, Maggie. Forget it," said Silvie.

"Do you want to sit with Brittney and me on the bus?" asked Maggie.

"Sure," said Silvie.

"It might have small seats," said Brittney immediately.

Silvie looked at the girls. They wore glittery shirts, bell-bottom jeans, and matching lip gloss. Silvie glanced down at her faded t-shirt and baggy jeans.

"Brittney's right. There might not be enough room," said Silvie.

"It'll be fine. We can talk about singing groups, or fashion, or boys. You know, girl talk," said Maggie.

Girl talk didn't sound like anything Silvie wanted to know about, think about, or talk about. She wished she was home with Millie. Gramps had let her pick out the cat from the Denver Dumb Friend's League. It was supposed to help her not miss Mama so much. Nothing really helped that but Silvie loved her fluffy kitty. The cat was missing part of her tail, and that was okay with Silvie since she was missing parts of herself, too. Millie didn't care about missing parts or the scars on Silvie's face. Even if the tabby could talk Silvie knew she would never say hurtful things.

"I see the bus!" yelled Adam in Silvie's ear.

Why do boys yell so much, wondered Silvie. Are they hard of hearing or do they want everyone else to be?

Silvie watched the loaf-of-bread-shaped yellow bus round the corner on 9th Avenue and slow to a stop. A few boys hooted. The accordion doors opened and a bald, square man moved from the driver's seat to the bottom step.

"Call me Curly," he said.

"Where are your curls?" blurted Adam.

"I left them somewhere," said Curly. "Now, listen up. No food, no candy, and no gum on my bus."

"Is he kidding? We'll starve," said Adam.

"I'm looking at you, wise guy," said Curly. "No yelling, no singing, and two to a seat. I'm retired from the U.S. Marine Corps, and I run my bus like junior boot camp. Any questions?"

"Tell this guy this isn't the Marines," said Adam.

"Hey, I heard that. You're sitting where I can watch you," said Curly.

Silvie chuckled. It seemed like Curly could handle Adam "The Brat" Westin.

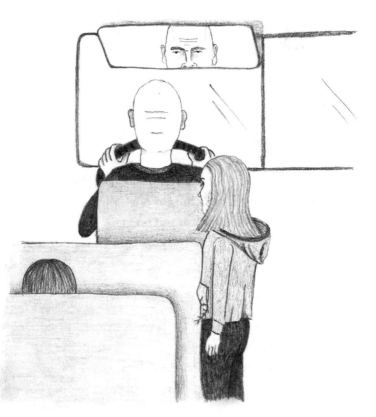

Silvie saw Brittney nudge Maggie with her elbow.

"I'm sorry, Silvie," said Maggie. "It's only two to a seat."

Silvie wasn't surprised, hurt, or shocked. She felt numb. It was the way she survived school every day.

"Don't worry about it, Maggie," said Silvie.

"Do you want some lip gloss?" asked Maggie.

"No thanks," said Silvie.

Kids shoved and cut in line ahead of her, but she didn't fight it. Silvie figured they were all jockeying to pair up and sit with their best friend, or second best friend, or third best friend. She had no best friend to worry about.

Silvie looked into the late March sky. An orange breasted robin, one of the first signs of spring, was flying low. The morning sun glared off the school windows and reflected the nearby tree branches like a mirror.

"It can't see the windows," whispered Silvie.

Thud! The bird hit a window and fell to the ground.

Silvie left the line and picked up the bird. She ran her index finger from its head to its tail.

"Your neck isn't broken; you're lucky. You're just in shock," said Silvie. "If I were home I could warm you up in a shoe box on the heat vent for a minute to bring you out of it."

"Come along, Silvie," called Ms. Crabtree.

Silvie carefully put the bird inside her fleece jacket and zipped it into hiding. She stepped to the back of the line and followed the kids onto the bus.

She walked down the aisle looking for an open spot and saw that every seat was taken.

"Sit down quickly," ordered Ms. Crabtree.

Silvie turned on one foot and saw Curly watching her in the big mirror above his steering wheel.

"We've got a front row seat for you up here, Missy," said Curly.

Silvie felt heat rising in her scarred cheeks as she headed back to the front of the bus.

I'm a ballerina walking across the stage, she imagined. "Of course they're all looking at me."

Silvie saw the open spot as she got closer to the front and noticed the top of the single head above the back of a seat.

"As soon as you're settled we start rolling," said Curly.

Silvie gracefully moved into the seat like a stray bead sliding onto a necklace string. She protectively put her hand on the small lump inside of her jacket.

Curly closed the accordion doors, started the engine, and put the bus into gear.

Silvie pressed back into her seat as it jerked forward. Only then did the ballerina turn her head to look at the student next to her. She would have welcomed a ghost over the person sitting there. Silvie sat face to face with Adam Westin!

Chapter 4

"Boo!" said Adam.

"You don't scare me," Silvie replied.

"I'm just getting you ready for the ghosts," said Adam.

"The only ghosts I know about are in your head," said Silvie.

"You'll see," said Adam, slumping down in the seat.

"You'll see that your dad is teasing you with his silly ghost stories," said Silvie. She dug in her pocket with her free hand. She found the folded paper with "Scrambled," the newspaper word puzzle, and pulled it out. She cradled the still lump in her jacket with her left hand. Suddenly the bus hit a bump, knocking Silvie sideways into Adam.

"Gross! I'm getting cooties," said Adam.

Silvie couldn't believe Adam still used that baby saying. "You are a cootie Adam, so how can you get them?"

"Just stay on your own side of the seat," warned Adam.

Silvie ignored Adam and unfolded her word puzzle. She would be glad to stay on her side of the seat. She didn't want to crush the near weightless bird hidden in her jacket. That last bump could have been disastrous.

Silvie studied the first of four jumbled words. N-A-S-T-E-P-L. She tried using the "L" to see if it triggered a word she knew.

I get Lepstan. That's not it. I'll try the "T" next. Now I get Tanslep. That's not it either. I'll try the "P". Maybe it's PL together. Yes! It's PLANETS.

Silvie wrote PLANETS in the boxes on the puzzle. She noticed that the "A" and the "N" were circled for use in the final answer to a riddle.

"What are you doing?" asked Adam, breaking Silvie's concentration.

"Nothing," she said.

"I don't care anyway," said Adam.

Silvie shrugged and looked back at "Scrambled." The second group of letters was EAWTR. She tried the "E" first and came up with EWART. No way

"Of course," she said to herself. "It's WATER."

She filled in the five squares and noted that the W and the R were circled.

"You are so boring. No wonder you don't have any friends," said Adam.

"I am not boring, and I do have friends," said Silvie.

"I've been in your class since kindergarten, Silvie. Trust me, you don't have any friends."

Silvie thought of Millie. Her cat was definitely her closest friend. There was Gramps, too. He was her family and friend all in one.

"Yes I do, they just don't go to this school," said Silvie.

"It's probably another one of your dreams like that picture you drew in third grade about wanting to be a ballet dancer when you grow up," said Adam.

Silvie looked out of the window as they passed a Greek restaurant and Smiley's Laundromat. Adam's words stung but not enough to keep Silvie from striking back.

"It was just as real as your picture of an astronaut."

"I'm not going to be a boring lawyer like my dad and grandpa. I will be an astronaut. Besides, you don't even take ballet lessons."

Adam wasn't giving in and neither was she.

"Well you don't take rocket flying lessons, do you?" asked Silvie.

"Not yet. I will when I'm older," said Adam.

"I'll take ballet lessons when I'm older, too," said Silvie, pulling her hair forward to cover her cheeks.

Silvie looked out the front windows of the bus. There were buildings packed together on either side of the street. The offices, restaurants, shops and apartment buildings formed solid canyon walls on either side of Colfax Avenue. Silvie had heard that it was the longest commercial street in the country going east to west. She could see the glint of a golden orb on the left in the distance. She knew it was the Colorado State Capitol.

Silvie focused back on her puzzle. The third group of letters was TAERH. The word EARTH jumped out at her. She smiled. Sometimes she got a word right away. She wrote it down, and noted that the "E" was circled.

"How's your puzzle?" asked Adam.

"Don't you have anything better to do than to interrupt me?" asked Silvie.

"I don't think so," said Adam. "You won't let people be friends with you even if they try! Don't be such a grump!" Adam turned and looked out of the window.

Silvie studied the back of his head. There was a funny cowlick in the top of his hair where it swirled into a circle. She couldn't think of even a short line of kids who wanted to be friends with her. Maggie tried to be nice, but she was usually busy with Brittney. Adam Westin regularly made a sport out of bugging her, and right now she felt like bugging him back.

"Don't be such a grump yourself," said Silvie.

"You're always mad because of your face," said Adam.

Silvie considered his comment for a moment. Mad is better than sad she thought. She wrote Adam's name on the side of her puzzle. She played with the letters.

"Your name spells MAAD."

"You're really twisted, Blake."

"No I'm not; but your name is definitely MAAD untwisted," said Silvie.

"Funny," said Adam, looking at Silvie's puzzle. "You're pretty good at rearranging letters. What's the last one?"

"I don't know. SOTSHG doesn't look like anything yet," said Silvie. I'll try TH first. THOGSS. That's not it."

"Try the H first," suggested Adam.

"Now we have HOGSST. Good one, Adam," said Silvie.

"Hogsst," repeated Adam. "I'm going to tell Josh he's a Hogsst next time he tries to eat his whole lunch in one bite!"

Silvie laughed. "That's sick."

"Yeah, but it's true," said Adam.

The bus stopped for a light at Colfax and Grant Street.

"Hey, there's the Capitol!" said Adam, pointing to the left.

Silvie saw the store fronts come to an end at the corner. Spacious, green lawn spread around the majestic, gray stone building covering a city block all by itself.

"You can see the gold dome," said Adam.

Silvie crouched down in her seat to see the top of the Capitol. It was definitely all gold.

"My dad says once there was a homeless man who panned gold from the water that ran off the dome through the gutters during rain storms. The ghosts that live here protect the gold from being stolen. I guess they felt sorry for the homeless man, so they let him get away with panning gold from the gutters," explained Adam.

Silvie thought about her walk to school earlier that morning and the beggar who called himself Dwayne.

"What happened to the homeless man?" she asked.

"The police asked him to stop," said Adam.

"The ghosts seem nice anyway if they felt sorry for the homeless man," said Silvie.

"I thought you don't believe in ghosts," said Adam.

"I don't, but you do," said Silvie. "Let's finish this word before we get off the bus. I'm trying G first."

"How about GOTHSS?" said Adam.

"That's not a word," said Silvie.

She wrote GHOTSS.

"I see it," she said.

"What is it?" asked Adam.

Silvie swallowed. "It spells GHOSTS!"

Chapter 5

"Is GHOSTS the only word it could be?" asked Adam.

"I think so," said Silvie. "It doesn't mean anything, Adam. Look, the two "S's" are in the circles. They're part of the final scramble to solve the riddle. It says, If you look you'll find the _ _ _ _ _ _ _ you seek."

The brakes squealed as they pulled to a stop in line behind an identical bus from another school.

"You can figure out the last part. It looks like about thirty other schools decided today was a good day for a field trip to the Capitol," said Adam.

Ms. Crabtree walked to the front. "Put your lunches in the big basket up here. Stay in line as you get off the bus." She looked at Silvie and Adam.

"No pushing, Mr. Westin," she said. "Let's go."

Silvie stuffed her word puzzle and pencil into her pocket. She would solve the riddle later.

She held her notebook and lunch in her right hand, and kept her left hand over the hidden bird. She stood up and felt a ripple.

"You're waking up. Good for you," she whispered.

Silvie dropped her lunch in the basket and stepped off the bus, trying not to jostle the passenger in her jacket. The rest of her class jumped, stomped, and tramped down the steps.

Silvie saw a hedge of bushes nearby on the lawn. Adam and Josh were play punching each other. She took a chance and quickly darted behind the hedge. She gently reached into her jacket and pulled out the bird. It looked at her with panicky black eyes.

"What are you doing?" hissed a voice.

Silvie spun around.

"Geez Adam! You almost gave me a heart attack!"

"Hey, where did you get that bird?" asked Adam, sticking his nose in her business again.

"It hit the windows back at school. I was keeping it warm inside my jacket until it came out of shock," said Silvie.

"You had that bird in your jacket all the way here?" asked Adam.

Silvie nodded.

"You sure are good at keeping secrets, Silvie. Can I hold it? If you let me, I won't tease you anymore. I promise."

Silvie didn't believe Adam Westin for a minute, but something within her shifted.

"Hold out your hand," said Silvie.

Adam held out his square, boy hand. Silvie noticed dirt under his finger-nails, but his open palm looked clean enough. She put the bird on its back in Adam's hand.

"It hardly weighs a thing," said Adam.

"Birds have hollow bones so they can fly easier," said Silvie.

"Why is it just lying there? Why can't it fly?" asked Adam.

"It can, but it won't while it's lying on top of its wings," said Silvie. "Tip your hand a little so it rolls onto its feet."

Adam tipped his hand, the bird rolled, and whoosh, it took off. The bird landed in a pine tree and looked down at the two kids.

"How did you know how to do that?" asked Adam.

"I saw some rangers banding migratory birds at Barr Lake one summer. That's how they released the birds. I never tried it myself until now," said Silvie.

"Everyone line up!" Ms. Crabtree's voice cut through the hedge.

"Let's go," said Silvie.

She and Adam slunk out from behind the shrubs. Adam jogged up to Josh.

Silvie looked across the street. She noticed an older man carrying a brief case, walking west on Colfax. He paused and looked at the group of school children making a racket louder than the Denver traffic. He seemed to be searching for someone.

Silvie couldn't help staring at the man. He looked right at her. He touched the brim of his hat with his finger, then he turned and disappeared behind some buildings.

Silvie followed her classmates up the long east sidewalk. The Capitol seemed enormous close up. The four identical, twenty-five-foot columns on the second floor made it look even bigger.

"Attention everyone," called Ms. Crabtree. "We are representing Dora Moore School now. Keep your voices down, stay with your partner, and remember to take notes for your field trip reports."

Silvie scanned the bobbing heads of her classmates. Bus partners shuffled to position themselves in pairs. Maggie waved at her and then locked arms with Brittney. Josh stood with his partner in front of Adam. That left Adam solo. Silvie couldn't believe her lousy luck. She had been in the same class as Adam Westin since kindergarten. He was like a pesky neighbor who wouldn't move away. At least he was trying to be nice today. She slowly walked over to him.

"I guess we're stuck together," said Silvie.

"Only when Crabtree's looking. We can do as we please the rest of the time," whispered Adam.

"Be careful doing as you please, Adam. I'm sure the ghosts will be watching your every move," warned Silvie. She couldn't resist teasing him.

"They only watch out for creeps who try to harm the Capitol," said Adam.

"What do the ghosts do if they catch them, jump out and yell, Gotcha?" asked Josh, cutting into the conversation.

"My dad says the ghosts play tricks on them like shining bright lights in their eyes so they can't see what they're doing," said Adam.

"Your dad seems to know a lot about this," said Josh. "Are you sure he's not a ghost, himself?"

"Very funny, Josh. He's just a boring lawyer who reads a lot about history and stuff," said Adam.

"It sounds like he makes up stuff and calls it history," said Josh.

"Sometimes he sees weird things when he's watching out of his office window," said Adam.

"Quiet," hissed Ms. Crabtree.

"Remind me to tell you the story about the airplane ghost later," said Adam.

Silvie nodded. While Adam is looking for ghosts I'll be looking for clues to the missing painting of President Lincoln, she thought.

Silvie moved with the line toward the steps. She looked into the windows on the first floor of the huge building but she couldn't see through them. Her eyes followed a stone column up to the second floor. More windows stared back at her. Motion in a middle window caught her eye and she saw the outline of a person. She squinted; it looked like a woman. Suddenly a bright flash hit Silvie's eyes. The light was the only thing Silvie could see.

Chapter 6

Silvie bumped into Adam.

"Watch it, Blake! You sure are clumsy for a ballet dancer," said Adam. "Or are you paying me back for running into you earlier?"

Silvie squinted at the parade of fifth graders bouncing up the steps.

"I guess the sun was in my eyes," said Silvie.

She followed her class up the stone steps into a large rectangular room. She scanned the portraits of stern-looking men on either side of the walls.

No one wanted to steal any of you, she thought. I wonder where the Lincoln portrait was hanging.

The room ahead beckoned visitors to come along on a journey back in time.

The older man at the information desk said, "Welcome everyone. I'm Mr. Weis. Let me know if you have any questions. You're a lucky group. You get Greta Rae as your guide today."

A sweet-faced woman with gray hair pulled into a loose bun approached the class.

"Good morning, children. Welcome to your state Capitol. This belongs to your parents, your teachers, your neighbors, and you. My name is Greta Rae, and I will be guiding your tour."

Silvie read Greta Rae M. Drawcrof on the woman's nametag. She dug into her backpack for paper and a pen. She flipped to a page in her notebook and wrote the guide's name. She planned to concentrate on getting information for her field trip report and the missing painting. It wouldn't matter that her partner was Adam and not Maggie. She intended to give Greta Rae her total attention.

"Boys and girls, we need you to use your quiet ballet feet today," said Greta Rae.

"That will be no problem for Blake," whispered Adam.

Silvie rolled her eyes. Actually it would be no problem for her.

"There are two hundred and fifty people at work in our Capitol, and we don't want to interrupt their meetings," said Greta Rae. "Now, who can guess how many floors there are in this building? The answer rhymes with the word "fix" and was the life boat number of the Unsinkable Molly Brown."

"Six!" called out Brittney.

"You're right. I'm very old-fashioned, so you'll have to raise your hands and wait to be called on from now on," said Greta Rae.

Silvie looked at Brittney, who stuck her tongue out at Silvie.

What does she have to be so grumpy about? Silvie wondered.

Greta Rae continued. "There is a basement below us. You're standing on the executive floor. The governor, lieutenant governor, and state treasurer have offices here. The legislature works on the second floor, and the third floor houses the presidents' portraits gallery. Our dome observation deck is at the top."

"I can't wait to go up there," whispered Adam.

Silvie nodded, but she was more interested in the third floor where the portrait disappeared. Maybe she, Silvie-the-self-appointed undercover detective, would notice a clue the police had missed.

"A man named Elijah Myers built our Capitol along with the Capitol buildings in Lansing, Michigan and Austin, Texas," said Greta Rae.

Silvie wrote 'Elijah Myers built Capitol' in her notebook.

"The building is made of gray colored granite which came from a quarry on Beaver Creek near Gunnison. Mr. Myers used Colorado materials for the building and the floor you're standing on. This floor is made from a stone that's named for the town the quarry comes from," said Greta Rae.

Silvie raised her hand along with three others.

"How about the girl in the back," said Greta Rae, pointing to Silvie.

"Is it marble?" asked Silvie.

"You're right. It is marble from Marble, Colorado near Aspen," Greta Rae replied.

Silvie saw Brittney roll her eyes.

"This marble was used in the Tomb of the Unknown Soldier in Arlington

National Cemetery and parts of the Lincoln Memorial in Washington D.C.," said Greta Rae. She held up a black and white stuffed bird. "Does anyone know the name of our state bird?"

"Do you know, Bird-Girl?" asked Adam.

"I think it's the Lark Bunting," said Silvie.

Adam called out, "Lark Bunting."

"You're right; but wait for me to call on you, young man. Remember, I'm old-fashioned," said Greta Rae.

Silvie liked Greta Rae. She was kind, even to Adam.

"Who saw our state flag outside?" asked Greta Rae.

All hands shot up. Silvie guessed everyone had seen the flag at one time or another even if they didn't see it today.

"Andrew Carlisle Johnson designed our flag, and it was adopted in 1911. The blue stands for the sky. The white stands for something that rhymes with glow, and we had thirty-six inches of it on March 19th in 2006" said Greta Rae.

"Snow!" said a few kids.

Greta Rae nodded. "It's actually for our snow-capped mountains. The C stands for Colorado. The circle in the center stands for our glorious golden sun, and the red symbolizes our reddish soil."

Silvie drew the Colorado flag in her notebook and labeled its parts.

"Behind us is a portrait of Roy Romer who served twelve years as our governor," said Greta Rae.

Mama had told her about the time she met Governor Romer at the Newsstand Coffee Cafe on 6th Avenue. The gentle eyes in his portrait seemed to stare at Silvie through the canvas. He looked a bit older than Governor Bill Ritter did today.

"Governor Romer is father of seven, grandfather of eighteen, and now a great-grandfather to hundreds of thousands of students since he has become superintendent of schools in Los Angeles," said Greta Rae.

"Wow!" whispered the kids in chorus.

"How many of you think Denver is the highest state Capitol?" asked Greta Rae.

Silvie raised her hand with the rest of the kids in her class.

"We are the third highest state Capitol city," said Greta Rae. "Cheyenne, Wyoming is 6,000 feet above sea level, and Santa Fe, New Mexico is 7,000 feet high. Denver is only a mile high at 5,280 feet, so that puts us in third place. Now follow me outside."

Silvie was alone at the back of the line as they walked to the west door. She turned to look at the portrait of Governor Romer one more time. The eyes had moved and they were staring right at her!

Chapter 7

"What's up with you, Blake? You look like you've seen a ghost or something," said Adam.

"I haven't seen any ghosts, Westin, have you?" Silvie replied.

"I think I saw the eyes on the portrait of Governor Romer following us," said Adam.

"Are you serious?" asked Silvie.

"Nope," said Adam, laughing. He playfully punched Silvie on the arm.

"You wacko!" said Silvie. For a moment she thought this must be what it's like to have a brother. Just when you think they're halfway decent, they do a boy-thing and drive you crazy. She saw Adam look back over his shoulder at Romer's portrait. Adam saw the eyes, too; she was sure of it; but he probably wouldn't admit it.

The class headed outside.

"Look at the fifteenth step, boys and girls," said Greta Rae.

Silvie positioned herself so she could see where Greta Rae pointed.

"In 1908 a plaque was placed here to mark the mile-high spot. It was stolen seven times since then," said Greta Rae.

"So the Lincoln painting isn't the only thing that has been stolen from the Capitol," said Silvie to herself.

"In 1947, the words, 'One Mile Above Sea Level' were carved into this fifteenth step. Then in 1969, it was decided that the eighteenth step was the real mile measurement, and so this brass marker was set into this step," Greta Rae explained.

Silvie looked at the marker along with everyone else.

"We now believe that the thirteenth step is the accurate 5,280 feet, mile measurement, and it has been so marked," said Greta Rae.

"Hey Blake, it's lucky thirteen," said Adam.

"I'm not superstitious about numbers, Westin," said Silvie. She wrote in her notebook that the thirteenth step was the mile marker.

"Turn half way around and you'll notice our Civil War Monument in front," said Greta Rae.

"What's that pencil-shaped thing?" asked Brittney.

"That's our Veteran's Memorial," said Greta Rae.

Silvie looked past the monument and memorial to the panoramic City and County Building. It looked like a scenic prop against the background of the Rocky Mountains.

"In the City and County Building we house the trial courts where judges and lawyers work," said Greta Rae.

"My dad and grandfather try cases there," said Adam.

"That's cool," said Silvie.

"It's time to head back inside," said Greta Rae.

Silvie and Adam brought up the rear and made their way into the building.

"This is pretty boring so far. It's just the regular history stuff," said Adam.

"I'm sure your ghosts are waiting for you somewhere here," said Silvie. "Personally, I am looking forward to seeing the presidents' portrait gallery where the Lincoln painting was stolen."

"Trust me, Blake. The ghosts are here. So, why do you care about the stolen painting?" asked Adam.

"I'm looking for clues. It's fun," said Silvie.

"Can I help?" asked Adam.

"We'll see," said Silvie.

"James W. Denver was the governor of Kansas, not Colorado. Who knows why our city is named Denver?" asked Greta Rae.

Adam raised his hand. "It's because Denver was once a part of the Kansas territory."

"Good for you," said Greta Rae.

"How did you know that?" asked Silvie.

"My dad's boring history habit," said Adam.

"Follow me, children," said Greta Rae.

Silvie looked up at the portrait of Governor Romer as they walked by. Although they had moved to a different spot, the eyes stared directly at her.

She glanced at Adam. He was looking up at the eyes, too.

"Our walls on the first floor are made of Rose Onyx. Almost all of the marble in the quarry was used right here on these walls," explained Greta Rae. "There are pictures in the marble. Can you see a nose, a chin, and a face of a famous president with the initials G. W.?"

Silvie watched Greta Rae trace the outline of a man's face in the rock.

"Is it George Washington?" asked Maggie.

"Right," said Greta Rae.

Silvie saw Brittney squeeze Maggie's arm.

"Look here," said Greta Rae. "Can you see a bison?"

Silvie nodded along with her classmates.

"What will you eat on Thanksgiving?" asked Greta Rae.

"Turkey," said the class in chorus.

"I see it," said Adam.

"Good," said Greta Rae. "There are actually three of them. Who can find the other two?"

Silvie watched Brittney and Maggie move to the front and trace the other two turkeys.

"Are you having fun?"

Silvie turned to look at the woman who spoke. Her name tag had Amy R. Cashe on it.

"Yes, thank you," answered Silvie. "We're looking for turkeys in the Rose Onyx."

"Greta Rae loves this part of the tour," said Amy. "She always forgets to point out my favorite picture. Can you see the dancer over there on the left?"

Silvie looked to where she was pointing. There in the marble wall was a ballerina holding out her graceful arms and standing on one toe.

"I see it," said Silvie.

"I'll bet you like to dance," said Amy.

"Yes, I do," said Silvie.

"I think you will be a great dancer one day," said Amy.

Silvie pulled her hair forward to hide her cheeks. She shrugged because she didn't know what to say. Maybe Amy hadn't noticed her scars; maybe she was just being polite and friendly.

"Come on, Blake," said Adam. "We're going."

Silvie looked for the dancer in the stone wall again, but she couldn't find it. She scanned the marble wall all over where she had just seen the figure. It was as if the rose colored swirls had moved into an abstract design. Silvie turned to ask Amy to point out the dancer again. She looked behind her, but there was no one there. The woman had disappeared.

Chapter 8

"Silvie, you're looking the wrong way again," said Adam.

"Did you see where the other guide went?" asked Silvie.

"There isn't any other guide. We have Greta Rae."

"Didn't you see me talking to a guide named Amy?"

"Oh, I get it. You're trying to make me think you were talking to someone who isn't there, like a ghost. Very funny, Blake."

Silvie looked at Adam. He seemed serious enough, but that didn't mean he wasn't joking. Silvie knew he would never keep his promise about not teasing her. She moved with the rest of her class behind Greta Rae. They were already in the habit of following her like ducklings waddling after their mother.

""Boys and girls, please have a seat on the floor facing the wall with the tapestry," said Greta Rae.

Maggie and Brittney sat together in front. Silvie, the ballerina, slid her right foot behind her body and folded herself into a sitting position in a single, flowing movement. She looked up at the hanging tapestry covering an entire section of the wall. The Rocky Mountains went across the top, and a river wound its way through the middle to the bottom. It was dotted with famous women from the past. Words bordered the tapestry.

"This piece of art took over 4,000 hours and more than 3,000 people to stitch by hand, said Greta Rae. The stitches are called crewel. Colorado's Apollo Thirteen astronaut, Jack Swigert, who is known for saying, 'Houston, we have a problem,' stitched on this tapestry with his mother. The football player, Rosie Greer, also stitched. All of the women on it are real. It is called Women's Gold because that was the miners' nickname for the yellow roses Margaret E. Crawford brought to Colorado in a covered wagon. Margaret used her daily water rations to keep the flowers alive all the way from Missouri to Colorado."

"She must have really loved those roses. Didn't she get thirsty using her water on flowers instead of drinking it?" asked Maggie.

"Yes, the thirst was terrible," Greta Rae replied. "It was so hot and dry. It took 34 days to get here from Missouri in that wagon. But it was worth every precious drop of water to bring the beauty of the yellow rose to the Rocky Mountains. There was a place where the trail became so narrow and steep everyone had to get out and walk."

Silvie noticed that Greta Rae had a faraway look in her eyes as she spoke.

"You talk like you were there," said Silvie.

"Oh really," said Greta Rae, looking a bit flustered. "I suppose when you study the past it is almost like being there yourself. Now, let's learn about some of these historical ladies."

"Get ready for the boring part," whispered Adam.

"You should be taking notes. How are you going to do your report?" asked Silvie.

"My dad will help me. He knows more history than Greta Rae ever will," said Adam.

"Suit yourself; but I'm listening, so hush," said Silvie.

Greta Rae started, "Chipeta, Chief Ouray's wife is on the top left. She tried to get the Native American Indians and the white men to be peaceful with each other."

Silvie wrote, "Chipeta worked for peace" in her notebook.

"On the upper right-hand corner there's Mother Cabrini who came here from Italy," said Greta Rae. "She was given a worthless piece of land for her school. She found a hidden spring on the land, built her school, and became America's first saint."

The nun, dressed in black from head to toe knelt on the ground by a heart-shape made of rocks. Silvie wrote, "Mother Cabrini finds water for her school." Underneath she wrote, "Mama, Lizzie Blake disappears in an explosion during the war." Silvie decided that if she made a tapestry it would have Mama and Gram on it. They were her heroes. She wrote, "Gram, Kate Blake, dies from AIDS caught while helping the sick in a homeless shelter." Silvie drew a heart made of rocks like Mother Cabrini's in her notebook.

"Boys and girls, in the middle there's Clara Brown and Ellen Jack," said

Greta Rae.

"Is that Aunt Clara Brown?" asked Adam.

"You're right, young man," replied Greta Rae. "Aunt Clara Brown was a freed slave who lived in Colorado's Central City."

"Why is Ellen Jack dressed like a cowboy with a gun?" asked Brittney.

"Captain Ellen Jack prospected for gold and silver in the mountains. It was rough back then," explained Greta Rae. "She had to protect herself."

Silvie wrote down the women's names and what they did. Most of the other fifth graders were taking notes. Adam was busy playing with an ant on the floor.

Silvie glanced across the room at an antique elevator. The ornate door was decorated in brass and surrounded by a carved wooden border. Silvie saw the brass arm at the top suddenly move along a half circle from 0 to 2. She knew the presidents' portrait gallery was on the third floor. Maybe the police were going to the floor underneath the gallery to look for more clues on the missing painting.

Greta Rae continued. "Helen Bonfils built Denver's Bonfils Theater. Mary Coyle Chase worked at the Rocky Mountain News and wrote Harvey, the play about an invisible rabbit, during the Second World War, to give Americans something to laugh about. She won the Pulitzer Prize and taught at the University of Denver."

Silvie laughed at the giant white rabbit holding hands with Mary. Helen Bonfils was the most stylish woman on the tapestry. She sat in the theater reading a newspaper.

"Touching the side of the theater is Mary Elitch Long," said Greta Rae. "Mary created Elitch Gardens, the amusement park."

"I've been there," said Adam. "I like

the roller coaster, and the Road Runner Express is a rush when it goes forward and then zips backwards!"

"No way; The Tower of Doom is the best ride ever!" said Josh.

Silvie looked at the elegant lady on the tapestry. She didn't think Mary Elitch Long would be up for the wild rides at Elitch Gardens today.

Silvie noticed the saloon dancer pointing her toe on top of a boulder near the bottom of the river. The figure wore a pink feather in her hair and a colorful, fitted sleeveless top with a long maroon skirt. She had netted gloves on her hands and arms held out at her sides. Silvie couldn't take her eyes off of the figure. She raised her hand.

"Can you tell us about the dancer?" she asked.

"That's Silver Heels. She's a mysterious one," said Greta Rae.

"She doesn't look mysterious to me," said Adam.

"Shhhh! I want to hear this," said Silvie.

"It's just because you like dancing," said Adam.

Silvie shot Adam a warning look. He shrugged. She didn't care if Adam thought she was a kook or not.

"Silver Heels made quite a name for herself as a dancer in the mountain mining towns, especially in a town called Buckskin Joe," explained Greta Rae. "When the smallpox epidemic hit many people died. Silver Heels took care of the sick until she got the disease herself."

She was like Gram. She caught the same disease that destroyed the people she helped, thought Silvie. "Did she die from smallpox?" Silvie asked.

"She didn't die, but the smallpox scarred her face and disfigured her," said Greta Rae.

Silvie reached up and touched her own scars. "When she got well did she start dancing again?"

"No; I'm afraid that Silver Heels went into hiding," said Greta Rae.

"She didn't want anyone to see her scars," whispered Silvie.

"For many years afterward, a woman wearing a heavy, black veil on her face was seen walking around the graves of those who died from the smallpox," said Greta Rae. "It was Silver Heels,"

"Or her ghost!" whispered Adam.

"Shush!" hissed Silvie.

"Silver Heels was very heroic," said Greta Rae.

Silvie nodded.

"Children, can you see the words to a famous song written around the border of the tapestry?" asked Greta Rae.

"It's America the Beautiful," said Maggie.

"Yes, it is. Kathy Bates came from Wellesley College in Massachusetts to teach at Colorado College. She climbed 14,000 feet to the top of Pike's Peak and was inspired to write this song. Let's all sing it now," said Greta Rae.

"Oh beautiful for spacious skies, for amber waves of grain," sang the fifth graders.

Silvie joined in. While they sang a worker came by and mopped the floor near the elevator. He finished and put up a yellow plastic sign. It was two-sided and connected at the top so it would stand like a tent. The words, 'Caution-Wet Floor' were printed in black on the sign. Silvie remembered the news had reported that two 'Wet Floor' signs were the only other things missing along with the Lincoln painting.

The children continued singing. "For purple mountain majesties above the fruited plain. America, America, God shed His grace on thee, and crown thy good with brotherhood from sea to shining sea."

The mopper clapped for them.

"Let's move to the rotunda," said Greta Rae.

Silvie's classmates noisily got to their feet. Silvie noticed the arm on top of the elevator moving from 2 to 0. She made her way to Greta Rae.

"Excuse me Greta Rae, but will we be allowed to ride the elevator?" Silvie asked.

"Oh no my dear," said Greta Rae. "That old thing hasn't worked in years!"

Chapter 9

"Too bad we can't ride that old elevator," said Adam.

"I saw the arm on top move. Somebody rode it from the basement to the second floor and back," said Silvie.

"No way! Maybe the arm just moves around the numbers even though the elevator doesn't work," suggested Adam.

"Why would the arm move by itself?" asked Silvie.

"It's probably the ghosts," said Adam, flatly.

"There's no such thing," said Silvie.

"Tell that to the ghost who was riding the elevator that hasn't worked for years," said Adam.

"This is getting a little weird," said Silvie.

"My dad says history is all about ghosts, and we're here in the middle of a bunch of them," said Adam.

It was more than Silvie could take. "I think normal things are happening, only they seem weird because you keep talking about ghosts," she said. "Let's just listen to Greta Rae."

They walked into a gigantic circular room with colorful murals on the walls. In the center was a twenty-step white marble grand staircase that ascended and then split into two opposing staircases continuing up on either side. The railing and sculpted posts were brass. Silvie looked up at the open ceiling rising through all the floors to the top of a dome.

"Children, you are standing in the rotunda," said Greta Rae. "The ceiling of this room is 180 feet high. That's eighteen stories tall. It's the same height as our nation's Capitol in Washington, D.C. You can see the north, south, and west wings from here. The east wing is tucked behind the grand staircase.

By now you've noticed the beautiful bronze balusters, railings and decorated columns. If you look carefully, you'll see the Colorado state seal etched into each of the brass doorknobs throughout the Capitol.

We have many exhibits and musical performances here during the year. Also, this room was used for Henry Cordes Brown who donated the land for this building, Governor Evans, and Buffalo Bill to lie in state before they were buried."

"That's disgusting," said Josh.

There were a number of groans from the fifth graders.

"I told you, Blake. This place is full of ghosts from the past," said Adam.

"Your head is filled with ghosts from the past, Westin," said Silvie. She wanted to get on with the tour so she could look for clues on the third floor. Her head wasn't filled with ideas about ghosts like Adam's, but rather with questions about who would want to steal a painting of Abraham Lincoln.

"These beautiful murals tell a story about the importance of water in Colorado's history," said Greta Rae.

Silvie saw a woman join the group. Her blonde hair was curled, and she looked stylish in her black dress and high heels. She reminded Silvie of one of the figures on the tapestry.

"Boys and girls, meet another guide and my friend, Nell Fishbone," said Greta Rae.

"Good morning, Nell," sang the kids in unison.

Silvie looked at the guide's name tag and wrote Nell Fishbone in her journal.

"Are you sure you want to be a dancer and not a secretary with all those notes you're taking?" said Adam.

"My father isn't a history buff," said Silvie. "I need something to help me write my report."

"Do you even have a father?" asked Adam.

"Nope, just a picture of Mama that he painted as a reminder that he was here," said Silvie.

"Was he an artist?" asked Adam.

"Gramps says he was more of a gold digger," Silvie replied. "He took off with a woman who owned a casino in Las Vegas. I never met the guy." She was surprised that she didn't mind telling Adam about her father.

"It sounds like you're better off without him," said Adam.

"That's what Gramps says," said Silvie.

Greta Rae's voice broke through their hushed conversation. "Nell will tell us about the murals."

"Throughout history," Nell began, "water has been important to Coloradoans. In the murals you can see how we used water in agriculture and in mining precious metals. From our early people, the Native American Indians seen in the first mural, to modern Coloradoans in the final painting the importance of this life-giving liquid is beautifully illustrated."

"Thank you Nell," said Greta Rae. "There are a few groups of children from other schools visiting the second floor right now, so we will go up to the third floor. Boys and girls, you must walk single file to the right side of the staircase so that others can come up and down," said Greta Rae.

Silvie took her usual place at the back of the line. She smiled at Nell. "Is it fun working here?'" she asked.

"Oh yes," replied Nell. "We get to meet lovely young people like your-selves. Do you like the murals?"

"They are pretty colorful," said Silvie. "Those miners in the mural look like they are working hard to find gold in the water."

"It was hard work, but some people got very lucky. Maybe you'll find a treasure yourself," said Nell.

"I don't think so," said Silvie.

"I'm sure if you look, you'll find the answers you seek," said Nell.

"That sounds familiar to me, but I can't remember why," said Silvie.

Nell smiled and winked at Silvie.

"You will," she said. "Enjoy the third floor."

Chapter 10

"I've been waiting to go to the third floor ever since we got here," said Silvie. "Bye Nell."

Nell Fishbone winked at Silvie before she turned and walked away.

Silvie took the grand staircase one marble step at a time, keeping her right hand on the brass railing. It felt smooth and cool under her sliding fingers. The brass posts gleamed, and as Silvie followed her class up to the landing she could see why. With soft white cloths, silent workers polished the circular posts and railings above them on each floor.

Silvie walked up the right side of the fork in the grand staircase. She noticed a woman in greenish-gray overalls methodically rubbing the bottom of a sculpted post. Silvie turned after she had passed and watched the woman wipe away fingerprints just left by the fifth graders of Dora Moore School.

"I bet the police didn't find any fingerprints after the Lincoln painting was stolen," Silvie told Adam.

"No kidding. They clean up fast around here," he said.

"Let's move to the Presidents' Gallery," said Greta Rae.

The group climbed a side staircase into a round room above the second floor rotunda. The center of the room was a huge, open circle at least forty feet across. A thick, chest-high brass railing served as a wall around the opening. The bronze posts were square at the bottom rising into Grecian vase shapes ending in rectangles where they connected to the railing. Two other women polished brass posts nearby. A lone police officer kept watch from the shadows of a doorway.

Silvie looked down into the rotunda. She was staring at the same 180-foot high opening that she had seen from below, but now she was two floors up in the middle of the vast space.

Silvie noticed that Josh and Adam had their heads together, looking down.

"Adam! Josh! Do not even think of spitting!" warned Ms. Crabtree.

"We aren't!" they said together.

Boys had some strange habits. Silvie saw Gramps spit once when he was working outside. She even tried it herself in the bathroom sink. It was a little bit like when she spit after brushing her teeth, but without a purpose. She moved closer to Adam.

"Did you do it?" asked Silvie.

"Nope," said Adam.

"Would you guys really spit in here?" she asked.

"We want to see who's spit is the fastest," said Adam.

Silvie knew the answer to that. Both drops of spit would fall as fast as each other and anything else. Once she had stood on her bed and dropped her hairbrush, a book and a quarter. They all landed at the same time. She wasn't Sir Isaac Newton, but that experiment proved to her that gravity pulls things down at the same rate regardless of their size or weight.

Adam grinned. "Do you want to spit with us when Crabtree isn't looking?"

"I'll pass," said Silvie. "Maybe you should wait and try it off the dome balcony when we're outside instead of in here."

"Good thinking, Blake!" said Adam.

"Cool," agreed Josh.

Silvie felt slightly powerful to think that she had talked Adam out of holding his spitting contest inside the Capitol.

"Boys and girls, look at the paintings," said Greta Rae.

Silvie faced the presidents' portraits. There were groups of four portraits bordered by plaster columns on each side. The columns turned to marble three-fourths of the way down to blend into the marble wall. Each column had a three-part fixture that threw light up onto the gold-framed paintings. The portraits were about two feet high by slightly less wide.

A person could carry one of these out easily enough, thought Silvie.

"As you all probably heard on the news, our collection of United States presidents' portraits is missing Abraham Lincoln today," said Greta Rae. "These portraits were painted by Lawrence Williams. The painting stolen yesterday was not the original. Our original painting of President Lincoln was taken in 1994."

Silvie jotted notes as Greta Rae spoke. "What was the difference between the original painting and the one that was stolen this week?" she asked.

"Ah, I see we have a young detective in the group," said Greta Rae, smiling. "Look closely. You'll see that all of the portraits have red signatures by the artist at the bottom, except for Jefferson."

"Thomas Jefferson has a black signature," said Adam.

"You are right, and so did the second portrait of Lincoln," said Greta Rae. "Lawrence Williams painted his signature in black only on the Jefferson and the second Lincoln," said Greta Rae.

"So the Lincoln painting that was stolen in 1994 was signed in red?" asked Silvie.

"That's correct, and it has never been found," said Greta Rae.

One of the women who was polishing brass slipped in behind Silvie while Greta Rae talked.

"Why would somebody want to steal Abraham Lincoln twice?" Silvie asked.

"That's a question that the police are trying to answer," replied Greta Rae. "Maybe if you look you can find the answers you seek and help the police solve the crime."

Silvie nodded. She wrote, "If you look you can find the answers you seek" in her spiral notebook. Nell had just said the very same thing to her. Silvie was sure she had heard or seen that saying even before Nell said it.

While her classmates wrote in their notebooks, Silvie went closer to the blank spot where the second Lincoln painting hung until the day before. There were no visible fingerprints or clothing fibers on the wall except for a dark mark at the top. Silvie figured the thief must have raised the painting from the bottom and scratched the wall with the top of the frame before lifting it off the hanger. That clue wouldn't solve anything, but she wrote it down anyway.

"Let's make our way to the side stairs," said Greta Rae.

Silvie's class moved with their guide.

Just then, the woman polishing brass turned to Silvie and said, "It's you."

"Excuse me," said Silvie. She read Revi Eshells on the woman's name tag.

"You are the one who can find the painting," said Revi.

"I was hoping to find some clues," said Silvie.

"There are clues all around you, Josie," said Revi.

"I'm sorry. You must have me mixed up with someone else. My name is Silvie," she said politely. She felt comfortable talking with Revi even though she was a stranger. Silvie didn't remember to pull her hair forward over her scarred cheeks.

"Of course you're not Josie. What was I thinking? Names are important. Silvie is a nice name. Is your mother with you?" asked Revi.

An ache filled Silvie's chest.

"My mother went to Iraq to help the wounded in the war. There was an explosion. She was lost. They sent us her I.D. tags," said Silvie.

A wave of emotion passed over Revi's face. "That is very sad. I'm sure you miss her. I had a daughter. You know, a mother's love lives forever in your heart," said Revi rubbing a dull spot on a post until it shone.

From the way Revi said "I had a daughter," Silvie figured something must have happened to her.

"What was your daughter's name?"

"I named her Josie," said Revi.

That must be why Revi called me Josie, thought Silvie. Schoolgirls probably remind her of her daughter.

"Josie's a nice name. I like the thing you told me about a mother's love," said Silvie quietly.

She wrote Revi's words in her journal so that she would remember. She also wrote, "Revi Eshells says names are important."

"Come on Blake," called Adam from the back of the line.

"I'm coming," said Silvie. "It was nice meeting you, Revi."

"It was a pleasure, believe me," replied Revi.

Silvie caught up with Adam. As she crossed the gallery she looked down to the second floor and noticed an opening with a large brass and wood door. It's the elevator from downstairs, thought Silvie, the one that Greta says hasn't worked in years. It was at that moment Silvie saw the arm on top of the elevator start to move once again.

Chapter 11

I could have imagined seeing that elevator arm move once or twice, thought Silvie, but not three times!

Silvie wouldn't normally walk away from her class on a field trip. She wouldn't normally disobey her teacher. She wouldn't normally care about an old elevator, but she was looking for clues to the stolen Lincoln portrait. Revi said she could find the missing painting. It was fun to think that she, Silvie Blake, could solve the mystery. She was actually starting to believe she could do it. Maybe, it was because she seemed to be the only one who saw the elevator arm moving or the only one who cared. She felt somewhere deep in her bones that the elevator was a clue.

Silvie walked down the stairs. She stepped boldly up to the elevator and pressed the button. Nothing happened. No light came on; no door opened.

"There you are," said Adam, coming up from behind her. "What are you doing?"

Silvie was almost used to being stuck with Adam by now. "I'm trying to get the elevator to work," she said.

"Why do you care about the elevator?" asked Adam.

"Maybe, it has something to do with the missing painting," said Silvie.

"Greta Rae says it hasn't worked in years. How can it be involved with the missing painting?" said Adam.

"I don't know, but there's something strange about it. I feel it," said Silvie. "I'm going downstairs to see if I can get the door to open on any of the other floors."

"Are you crazy? You're going to get into big trouble," said Adam.

"You should go back with the class. I'll catch up. This won't take me very long," said Silvie.

"No way, Blake. I'm coming with you. We're partners, remember?" said Adam.

Silvie didn't care if Adam came with her, but she didn't want to be responsible for his fate with Ms. Crabtree.

"We'll be in trouble if we get caught," said Silvie.

"It may be the first time for you, but it won't be the first time for me," said Adam. "Besides, it will be more interesting than some old cannon balls from the Mexican War welded onto the staircase posts that Greta Rae is talking about. Let's go. We can catch up with everybody before they head to the dome," he said.

"Okay. We know where the elevator is on the first floor. Let's try the buttons," said Silvie.

As Adam followed her to the grand staircase Silvie saw Revi coming toward them.

"Did you lose something?" asked Revi.

"Do you know anything about this elevator?" asked Silvie. "Does it work?"

Just then one of the other brass polishers walked by and said, "Come on, woman, we need to polish the railings by the Supreme Court room. There's no time to chat."

Silvie looked into Revi's eyes.

Revi winked and walked off with the worker coaxing her to her next task.

"Did you see that? She winked when I asked about the elevator. That means Greta Rae is wrong. The elevator works. Let's go," said Silvie.

"Do you know that lady?" asked Adam.

"Not really. I just met her; why?" said Silvie.

"I don't know. It seems like you know her, or she knows you," said Adam.

"Next you'll be telling me that Revi is one of your ghosts," said Silvie.

"Or one of yours," said Adam quietly.

"Come on," she said.

Adam followed her down the grand staircase and across the floor surrounded by giant murals. They walked quickly to the antique elevator door.

"Push the button," said Silvie.

Adam poked the button with his index finger. They waited, but nothing happened.

"Let me try it," said Silvie. She pushed the button, but again, nothing happened. She looked up. The elevator arm pointed to zero.

"It's stopped at the basement. Let's go down one more floor and try it," said Silvie.

She took Adam by the arm and was running before she thought about it.

They found their way to the brass railed staircase and took it to the lowest level. They flew over the steps and landed on the marble basement floor. Pillars and posts dotted the room. There were tables and a glass counter filled with snacks. The chandelier above their heads looked too fancy for a basement.

Silvie figured that this area would generally be crowded, but since the Capitol was closed to the public today, it was deserted. There was no one there to notice a couple of school age children wandering around the basement unsupervised.

"There's your elevator," said Adam, pointing to the right.

The basement elevator door was not ornate like the first and second floor doors. It was plain metal, painted light green to match the walls.

Silvie walked up to the elevator and pushed the button on the wall next to the door. They waited. Nothing happened.

"It doesn't make sense," said Silvie. "This has to work in order for the arm to move. Somebody just rode it down here because the arm stopped on the 0."

"It's the ghosts," said Adam.

"You know I don't believe that," said Silvie.

"I'm sure the ghosts who are riding that elevator don't care if you believe in them or not," said Adam.

"There has to be a logical explanation," said Silvie.

"We'd better get back upstairs with the class," said Adam.

"I need one minute more," said Silvie.

Silvie put her hand on the door. It felt cold and still. She looked all around the top of the frame and where the tile floor met the metal door. It was there in the space between the bottom of the elevator door and the floor that something caught her eye.

Chapter 12

Twenty-three blocks from the Capitol Dwayne Beasley sipped coffee from a paper cup some "do-gooder" bought for him at the near-by convenience store.

"This is so you won't waste money on something that's not healthy for you," said the plump, curly haired woman.

"Thank you, ma'am," said Dwayne, to keep from saying that he was old enough to know what was healthy for him or not. Since he had no choice in the type of beverage he was given, he decided that even beggars deserve a coffee break now and then. He sat down on a concrete curb and let the hot liquid warm him.

Today had turned out differently than Dwayne planned. If only the new homeless woman had been right, he thought. I might have the fortune in my hands right now. I could get a real hotel room, and some clothes, and sit at a real bar and order something stronger to drink than coffee.

Dwayne went back over yesterday's events in his mind. He had taken the little silver key off the chain on her neck while she napped. It was her fault for telling him her stories anyway. She said the key led to a treasure and could unlock the door to riches. She told Dwayne about the opening to the underground tunnel near the viaduct and that the tunnel led to the basement of the Colorado State Capitol. She said at the end of the tunnel there was a door that the key unlocked. She said there was a riddle hidden in the back of the Lincoln portrait, and whoever solved it would be rich.

Then she forgot she had told him any of it. Many of the homeless were mentally ill. You could never count on them.

Dwayne should have known better, but he didn't. That's why he took the key and went looking for the opening to a tunnel near the viaduct. That's why he went down the tunnel all the way to the door and opened it with the key. That's how he found himself inside of an old elevator with a door that opened to the front and back, and how he rode it to the top. That's how he ended up on the second floor and saw the paintings up on the third floor through the opening above the staircase. That's how he waited until no one was looking and lifted the Lincoln portrait off the wall, hid it between two "Wet Floor" signs, and got back on the elevator without anyone noticing. That's how when the elevator opened on the basement floor side with the tables he used the key to close the door and open the tunnel side.

The tunnel was dark, so he waited until he got to the campsite to look behind the painting. He couldn't find a riddle or anything else. Then, when he went to put the key back on her neck it was gone, somewhere between the tunnel and the basement of the Capitol. He put the Lincoln portrait near her instead.

Dwayne hoped that when she woke she would like seeing the painting of President Lincoln at the campsite. He hoped she wouldn't notice that the key on her necklace was missing. Ever since the beginning, when she showed up out of nowhere one day, she would forget the things she said after she said them. He hoped the key would be like that, and she would forget about it too.

Chapter 13

In the Capitol's basement Silvie bent down and pulled at the object sticking out from under the elevator door. It was metal and silver like the edge of a nickel. It wouldn't move.

"It's stuck," she said. "It looks like a silver coin."

"Try to pry it loose with your pen," said Adam.

"Good idea," said Silvie.

She poked the pointed end of her pen next to the object and worked at the edge until it started to slide out from under the door.

"I've got it!" Silvie said, pulling it out.

"It's only a key," said Adam.

"Whose is it, and what does it open?"

"I have no idea. Let's go back."

Silvie wasn't ready to go quite yet. She studied the elevator door.

"Wait. There's a keyhole by the buttons," said Silvie.

"You really do act like a detective. Go on, Blake, try it," said Adam.

Silvie aimed the key at the opening and pushed. It wouldn't go in. She rotated the key a half turn and tried it again. This time the key slipped into the hole like a hand in a glove. She turned it to the right. Nothing happened. Then she turned it to the left. Suddenly, iron gears groaned as metal turned against metal and the elevator door slowly opened.

"Whoa!" exclaimed Adam.

"Can I offer you a ride to the second floor?" asked Silvie.

"You bet!"

Silvie took the key, and they hopped into the elevator.

"You don't think we'll get stuck in this thing, do you?" said Adam.

"You can take the stairs. I'll try it.

If I get stuck call the fire department," said Silvie.

Adam thought for a second. "We're partners; we go together."

Silvie didn't know where she was getting this pulse of courage and adventure. Maybe it was from so many years of training herself not to care about what other people thought or said. Maybe it was from hearing about all the heroic women on the tapestry, and maybe it was coming from the spirits of all the people who had something to do with this historic building.

Inside the elevator, Silvie put the key into its spot on the panel and turned. The door closed. She pushed the button by the 2 and felt the world rising as the old elevator slowly creaked upward. A few seconds later the elevator bumped to a stop, and the door opened.

They stepped out onto the second floor. A sign with an arrow pointing left read, "Senate Chambers." Another sign with an arrow pointing right read, "Old Supreme Court Chambers-Room 220." A few of the presidents' portraits were visible above through the 180-foot-tall opening to the rotunda. Silvie looked around. There was no one there except for a single brass polisher.

Revi stared right at her. Silvie recognized the look on her face. She had seen it on Mama's face many times. It was pride or something close to it. Silvie was certain of it.

"Silvie! Adam!" called Ms. Crabtree from around the marble wall.

Silvie reached into the elevator and grabbed the key. The door closed as Ms. Crabtree stomped around the corner.

"What are you doing? Why aren't you two with the group? Didn't I tell you not to wander off?" drilled Ms. Crabtree.

Silvie knew that as long as she kept firing questions at them one after another, they wouldn't have to answer any of them.

"Now, come along. We're up these stairs in the room where the state legislators have their meetings," continued their teacher.

Ms. Crabtree marched forward. Silvie and Adam fell in line and followed.

Silvie glanced over her shoulder at Adam. He walked like a tin soldier without bending his knees and crossed his eyes at her. She controlled a giggle, but couldn't hold back the grin spreading on her face.

Ms. Crabtree led them up a narrow, concrete stairway with bronzed cannon balls welded to the top of each post. Silvie put her hand on one of the cannon balls as they passed. It was about the size of an orange and fit in her hand like a baseball.

Adam took hold of a cannon ball and pulled himself toward it until it touched his chest. He hung his tongue out to the side and fell onto the stairs. Silvie laughed. Ms. Crabtree spun around, but Adam had already popped up again. Their teacher glared at her two wayward charges. Adam appeared completely innocent. Silvie cleared her throat and pressed her lips together tightly to keep from cracking up. Ms. Crabtree turned and continued onward.

"You're a kook!" Silvie mouthed to Adam.

At one of the landings they followed Ms. Crabtree out onto a hallway covered with lush, maroon carpet. The other end of the hall led them into a long rectangular observation deck with huge windows on one side. Through the windows Silvie saw a gigantic room that looked like a theater. She spotted Maggie and Brittney with their noses pressed to one window. The rest of the kids were focused on an object being discussed by Greta Rae.

"You can see the one-ton, or 2000-pound, crystal and brass chandelier that hangs in what used to be the Supreme Court room. The highest court in our state used this beautiful room from 1894 until 1977. Today the 65 state representatives hold meetings and make decisions here."

Silvie looked through a window into the old Supreme Court room. Beneath the massive light fixture were chairs facing a wall-length wooden desk. Microphones poked up at every seat.

"The names of our state representatives appear on the backs of their chairs," said Greta Rae. "Also, notice Chief Ouray along with the others, part of our heritage, in the colorful stained glass windows."

"When do we get to go to the dome?" asked Adam.

"There's something you need to know about the dome," responded Greta Rae.

Chapter 14

Everyone stared at Greta Rae.

"The dome has been closed to the public for security reasons since the 9-11 tragedy," she said.

Disappointed groans moved like an ocean wave across Silvie's classmates.

Greta Rae continued. "But we recently reopened it, and I've been given permission to take you up there. Follow me." Greta Rae headed back toward the concrete stairway.

The kids cheered and fell in step behind her. Silvie stuck her hand into her jeans pocket. She touched the elevator key.

As if Adam read her mind he whispered, "Do you think the key has something to do with the painting?"

"Maybe the thief took the painting and then rode the elevator to the basement. But how did he walk out of the building without being seen?" said Silvie.

"It doesn't make sense," said Adam.

Greta Rae announced, "There are 93 steps to the dome, children."

Josh punched Adam's arm. "We'll never make it!" he said.

"It'll be a piece of cake," boasted Adam.

The stairs grew narrower and steeper as they walked. In spite of the "Whisper Only" rule, the kids' voices echoed in the cement stairway.

Concrete steps merged into black iron stairs. They were the kind that looked like they were hanging in mid-air. Silvie remembered being frightened of steps like these, but they didn't bother her today. Suddenly she heard a fuss at the front of the group.

"I can't go up these!" screeched Brittney.

"Don't be scared, Brittney," said Maggie.

"Go up or move over," called Josh.

"Come on, Brittney, you don't want to miss the dome," said Ms. Crabtree.

Silvie felt a jolt of courage and moved toward the commotion.

"Brittney, I know these stairs are creepy."

Brittney had a wild look in her eye like the bird that Silvie had caught earlier before it realized that it was free to fly away.

"Focus straight ahead and keep your hand on the railing," said Silvie. "Maggie will walk next to you, and I'm behind you. I won't let you fall backwards."

Brittney frowned. Silvie knew Brittney was considering her offer.

"We can stop any time you want. Let's just try three steps."

Brittney nodded, and took Maggie's hand.

Silvie tucked her spiral notebook in the back waistband of her jeans and slid her pen over her right ear. She did not cover her scarred cheeks with her hair. It occurred to her that she had less time for that old habit in the last few hours. She grabbed the railing with her left hand and put her right hand on Brittney's shoulder. The girls moved up three steps and stopped.

"Can you go up three more steps, Brittney?" Silvie asked.

Brittney slowly nodded. It was in this fashion that the trio climbed the final steps and came out into a circular room with a railing around the center. Brittney looked slightly green, but she managed a weak smile. Her blonde bangs were pasted to her forehead with sweat.

Adam gave Silvie the thumbs-up sign. Silvie joined the others at the railing and glanced down 180 feet to the bottom of the marble steps on the grand staircase. It looked more like 500 feet.

"You don't have to look over the railing, Brittney," said Silvie.

Greta Rae was lecturing again. "There are sixteen stained glass windows up here like that one of Kit Carson. Now, let's proceed onto the observation deck."

The fifth graders separated, pushed, and squeezed out of the multiple doorways leading to the outside deck. Silvie took Brittney's free hand, as she and Maggie gently moved Brittney outside.

"You can see the whole city of Denver from up here," said Greta Rae. "The gold dome is an umbrella between us and the Colorado sky."

Silvie took in the view. She saw tops of houses and office buildings. The gigantic City and County Building looked as if it would fit in her hand from up here, and she felt like she was level with the front range of the majestic Rocky Mountains. The streets below resembled the teeth of a comb with Colfax Avenue as the handle.

"I can see the red roof of my family's law office from here," said Adam.

"Where?" asked Silvie.

"The big street to our left is Broadway. Look at the next street to the right and then down about three inches," said Adam.

"I see it!" said Silvie.

"I'm supposed to work there when I grow up," said Adam.

Greta Rae started again. "Our dome is covered with 24-carat gold leaf. It has to be redone after heavy rain and hail storms when the gold flakes off."

"How much is the dome worth?" asked Adam.

"I don't know, but it cost $224,000 to repair in 1991, after a hail storm," said Greta Rae.

"That's expensive storm water running off this dome," said Adam.

"You bet it is! Let's head downstairs. It's about time for your picnic lunch on the lawn," said Greta Rae.

"No wonder that homeless guy was panning gold in the drain pipes off this roof," said Silvie.

Adam nodded.

Silvie took Brittney's arm. "We'll go down the same way we came up. Keep looking straight ahead. We'll be there before you know it."

The herd of noisy kids was soon at the bottom of the grand staircase with Brittney, Maggie, Adam and Silvie bringing up the rear.

"We all owe Greta Rae our sincere thanks for a wonderful tour," said Ms. Crabtree.

"Thank you Greta Rae," sang the fifth graders. Silvie wondered how many of this old building's secrets Greta Rae knew. She looked down the great staircase into the basement where she spotted a custodian mopping the tile floor near a closed door across from the elevator.

"Does that door down there have a state seal on its handle too?" asked Silvie.

Greta Rae moved to look where Silvie pointed. "Oh no, dear that door closes off one of the old tunnels."

"Did you say tunnels?" asked Silvie. "There are tunnels under the Capitol?"

"Yes," said Greta Rae. "Most people aren't interested in them. There are about 90,000 square feet of tunnels running under this building."

"Where do they go?" asked Silvie.

"Some of them connect us to other official buildings. Some supply energy to the Capitol. There's one tunnel down there that was used in the late 1800's to bring in coal," said Greta Rae.

Silvie let Greta Rae's words paint a picture in her imagination of a network of hidden tunnels. "That's interesting. Thank you Greta Rae."

Silvie followed her class outside. Ms. Crabtree had already retrieved the bucket from the bus and was passing out lunches. Silvie got hers and took a bite of peanut butter, mayo, and dill pickles on wheat bread. As she chewed she thought about tunnels leading in and tunnels leading out, and the elevator that didn't work, unless you had a certain key.

Silvie watched Adam and Josh flipping a coin while they ate. Boys! Why couldn't they just sit and eat their lunches like normal people? She listened to Adam say, "Call it, heads or tails."

Silvie thought about heads and tails, tops and bottoms, fronts and backs. Her mind locked onto a possibility. She rewrapped her sandwich and stuck it back into her bag. She stood up.

"Where are you going, Blake?" asked Adam.

Silvie hesitated and said, "I'm going to the restroom."

Adam resumed his coin flipping with Josh as Silvie walked up the stone steps. Suddenly, Adam was at her side.

"I told Crabtree you were going to the bathroom. I'm going with you," said Adam.

"You're going with me to the bathroom?" said Silvie.

"Is that really where you're going?" asked Adam.

Silvie took a deep breath. "Nope, I'm going back to the elevator."

"Why?" asked Adam.

"I want to look inside," said Silvie.

"What are you looking for?" asked Adam.

"Come on and you'll see," said Silvie.

"Are you kids going to the restrooms?" asked the man at the information desk.

"Yes; thanks, Mr. Weis," said Silvie, reading his name tag.

At the top of the grand staircase, Silvie looked up and saw Revi polishing a brass post. Silvie waved. Revi smiled and waved back.

Silvie and Adam zipped down the steps into the basement. It was empty like before. Silvie reached into her pocket and pulled out the key. She slipped it in place and turned. The elevator door opened. She and Adam stepped inside. Then, Silvie used the key to close the door.

"Now what?' asked Adam.

"Turn around," said Silvie, moving with him. Silvie found what she was looking for. She slipped the key into a hole near the back wall. She turned the silver key. The back wall hummed and then moved. The fact that it was a door now became visible as it slowly creaked open. Beyond it was a dimly lit tunnel.

Chapter 15

"Awesome, Blake! How did you know?" said Adam.

"I didn't know for sure, but when Greta Rae talked about underground tunnels I started to wonder where they were," explained Silvie. "Besides, I couldn't get this elevator out of my mind."

"Do you think the thief used this tunnel to steal the painting?" asked Adam.

"Maybe," said Silvie. Her feet shuffled forward on the concrete floor.

"You may be shy, but you're not a scaredy cat!" said Adam. "I guess we're going in the tunnel."

"Yeah, I guess so," said Silvie. She couldn't believe her own bravery. The tunnel was barely lit by the open elevator. It would be dark in another few yards. She didn't mind that Adam was right behind her now.

"How far are we going, Blake?"

"A couple more steps. I can hardly see," said Silvie. "It smells down here."

"Yeah, it smells like mice and something else," agreed Adam.

"Let's not even guess what else," said Silvie.

"We can't turn back yet," said Adam.

Silvie knew that if she was with Maggie or Brittney down here they would have never gone this far. Adam had been a lucky choice for her partner today after all. They shuffled side by side now, feeling the floor with their feet.

"This must be how a blind person feels," said Silvie. She let her hand lightly graze the wall to keep her bearings.

"There's some kind of metal track here on the ground," said Adam.

"I feel it, too," said Silvie. "It must be one of the tracks Greta Rae said was used to deliver coal to the Capitol."

"I wish we could see," said Adam.

Silvie was sure they could go no farther as her eyes worked to focus. Suddenly she saw a haze ahead. Was she imagining it?

"There's light up there," said Adam. "Just in time, too."

"The opening could be up there," said Silvie. She pointed even though it was too dark to see her own finger.

As they shuffled forward the light grew brighter. It illuminated millions of dust particles mixed with miller moths.

"These are the first moths I've seen this spring," said Adam.

"This tunnel is warmer than the outside. That's probably why they come out early in here," said Silvie.

"I'm sure there are a few other things living here, too. We just can't see them," said Adam.

"Yup," said Silvie. She didn't want to think about it. Something silky grazed her forehead. "Yeesh!" she hissed. "I just ran into a spider web!"

Adam had curved his arms up over his head shielding himself from the moths and webs. Silvie did the same.

After a few more steps the opening was visible.

"It's a brick wall," said Adam.

"Some bricks are knocked out," said Silvie. "There's a board or something covering part of it." Silvie peeked through the hole. "I see grass, and I can hear running water." She poked her head out of the opening. No one was near. "Let's go."

They climbed out and stood in the dirt. Car tires rolled overhead.

"Where are we?" asked Silvie.

"I think we're under the viaduct, probably near Speer Boulevard," said Adam.

A bicyclist whizzed by on a path below them.

Silvie surveyed the scene. It included two trash cans, a shopping cart, three sleeping bags, and a few rolled up blankets. "It looks like a campsite."

"It is," said Adam. "Homeless people are always camping out under these bridges. My grandfather complains about it all the time."

"Do the homeless people hurt anybody?" asked Silvie.

"Naw; they just beg out on the street," said Adam.

Silvie thought about the man with the sign she saw earlier. "I saw a beggar on the way to school today. I gave him some change."

"Don't be surprised if you see him again since you gave him something," said Adam.

"It wasn't very much," said Silvie. She didn't mind that the man needed money. She didn't mind saying good morning and giving him her spare change. She did mind that he said he knew her. She put it out of her thoughts.

"Don't the homeless people worry about leaving their stuff out here?" she wondered out loud.

"It's all junk. Nobody would take it. Besides, my grandfather says that most of these people are mentally ill anyway. They probably don't remember if they have a blanket or not."

"That's sad."

"I guess it is."

"I've seen a few people pushing shopping carts through our back alley. They dig in the trash dumpsters," said Silvie. "I guess they sleep here."

In one brimming shopping cart there was a pillow, a lamp with a broken shade, a dozen empty soda pop cans, and some worn boots.

"See what I mean?" said Adam. "This is all junk."

Silvie stepped around the shopping carts to the pile of sleeping bags and blankets. "At least they have sleepovers with friends every night," she said. Something inside her rumbled like clouds moving through her chest. She had never been invited to a sleepover, nor did she have a girlfriend to invite to one.

An object sticking out of one of the blankets caught Silvie's eye, snapping her back to the present. "There's something behind those blanket rolls," she said.

"Where?" asked Adam.

"Up against the concrete wall over there," said Silvie.

Normally Silvie wouldn't pry into other people's business. Normally she wouldn't be at a homeless people's campsite. Normally she wouldn't have a partner, and normally she wouldn't feel this bold. Actually, there was nothing normal about today.

Silvie stepped carefully over the bedding and lifted the corner of the blanket. A solid, gold edge peeked out. She heard Adam gasp. She pulled the blanket back and watched the object grow into a medium-sized gold picture frame. In the center was a painting of Abraham Lincoln!

Chapter 16

Adam was at her side reaching for the painting.

"Don't touch it!" warned Silvie.

"Why not?" asked Adam.

"You don't want your fingerprints on it," said Silvie.

Adam pulled his hand back. "I knew that."

Silvie moved the blanket away from the bottom edge of the portrait. "The artist signed in black," she said. "Greta Rae told us that the first portrait taken in 1994 was signed in red. This is definitely the painting of Lincoln that was stolen yesterday."

"Should we bring it with us?" asked Adam.

Silvie thought for a moment. "I think a crime scene should be undisturbed," she said. "Let's leave it here and let the police know where to find it. If we bring it back they might think we had something to do with stealing it. Besides, we can't tell anybody how we got here."

"Hey, you kids, freeze right there!" yelled someone.

Silvie looked over her shoulder. A man was running toward them.

"That stuff belongs to us!" he called.

Silvie and Adam leaped over the blankets and scooted for the tunnel. The man was half running, half hobbling. "I'll get you, you hoodlums!" he yelled.

Silvie pushed Adam ahead of her into the tunnel and scampered after him. They talked as they cruised through the tunnel.

"That guy thought we wanted their blankets," said Adam.

"He didn't seem like he was going to give us a chance to explain anything," said Silvie.

"Do you think he took the portrait?"

"I don't know; maybe he did. We should be getting back to the class anyway."

"Those homeless folks have great taste. They have a bunch of junk and a portrait from the state Capitol. Why would they take it?"

"It doesn't make any sense. Maybe the thief left it in some alley, and one of them found it."

Silvie felt more confident traveling through the tunnel now. Adam seemed more at ease too. They started running toward the light from the open elevator.

The reality of getting back to the lunch group suddenly hit Silvie. "Let's not say a word about this to Ms. Crabtree," she said. "She will be so mad that we left the class again."

"How are you going to tell the police about the portrait without Crabtree knowing?" asked Adam.

Silvie stopped inside of the elevator and thought for a moment. "I could write a note and slip it on the front desk as we leave after lunch. I'll make sure nobody sees me. It will tell the police where to look for the missing painting. Or, we could make a phone call from a pay phone on the way home after school."

"The phone call sounds safer. Hey, Blake, you sure know how to make a boring field trip a whole lot more exciting!" said Adam.

Silvie felt an unfamiliar lightness. She shrugged, but she was smiling. She found the key in her pocket and slipped it into the keyhole on the back door of the elevator. It closed, securing them inside. She turned to the front door and put the key in place.

"Which floor are we going to?" asked Adam.

Silvie didn't have to think long about her response. "I think we'd better get out here in the basement and run upstairs. We'll have less chance of getting caught," she said.

Adam nodded.

Silvie turned the key and the front door slid open. She and Adam were suddenly standing face to face with a stern woman in a gray uniform. There was a silver badge on her chest. The words "Security Guard" were stitched in gold thread onto her shirt.

Chapter 17

"Well, what have we here?" asked the guard.

Silvie grabbed the key and stepped out of the elevator. Adam followed right behind her.

"We wanted to ride the old elevator," said Silvie, truthfully. "I hope we didn't cause any trouble, Ms....." Silvie looked at the guard's name tag. It said Captain Jen Leckal. "I mean Captain Leckal," finished Silvie.

"This old elevator doesn't work," said Captain Leckal.

Adam looked frozen like a statue. Silvie thought fast. She chose her words carefully.

"We were told it doesn't work. We got the door to open somehow, and we tried to ride it up and down." Silvie stopped there to prevent herself from lying.

"Well, I take it you've figured out the truth and satisfied yourselves," said Captain Leckal.

"Oh yes Ma'am, we did," said Silvie.

"Yes Ma'am," echoed Adam.

"There's no harm done then. I have to take you back to your class. We like our field trip groups to stay together you know," said Captain Leckal.

"Our class is on the west lawn having a picnic lunch," said Silvie.

"Come along," ordered Captain Leckal, heading for the stairs. "I'll send maintenance down here to look at that elevator door."

Silvie glanced at Adam and then at the open elevator door. She still had the key hidden in the palm of her hand. She stuck it in the keyhole on the outside of the elevator, turned it once, and then slipped it into her pocket.

The elevator door closed noisily, but Adam and Silvie were already bounding up the stairs behind Captain Leckal.

The security officer led them swiftly across the marble floor. Silvie felt small comfort when she saw Revi polishing a post near the bottom of the grand staircase. They passed close enough for Silvie to hear Revi's voice.

"The key opens more secrets. Keep looking," Revi said.

Silvie frowned. She had found the stolen painting. What other secrets were there?

"What do you mean?" whispered Silvie.

"Ask your father about the first painting of Lincoln," said Revi.

Silvie was jarred by Revi's words. Should she tell Revi that her father had left before she was born? What did the father she never knew have to do with a portrait of Abraham Lincoln stolen in 1994?

"I've got to go," said Silvie.

Silvie caught up with Adam and Captain Leckal. She saw Adam grab a few brochures about the Capitol from the information desk.

"Help yourself," said the man sitting there.

"Thank you, Mr. Weis," said Silvie.

"Our alibi," said Adam holding up the brochures.

Captain Leckal headed out onto the sprawling lawn facing the Rocky Mountains.

Adam grabbed Silvie's arm. "Did you see the portrait of Governor Romer?" he asked.

"Not just now, why?" said Silvie.

"The eyes were watching us. There are ghosts here, Blake. I'm sure of it!" said Adam.

Silvie shook her head. Now she knew that Adam, too, had noticed the Governor's eyes in the painting.

As Adam and Silvie stepped outside, Ms. Crabtree was on her feet in a flash making a beeline for them.

"We have something more real than ghosts to worry about at the moment," said Silvie, taking a breath and bracing herself.

"Adam! Silvie!" blared Ms. Crabtree, as if it were all she needed to say.

"We apologize, Ms. Crabtree," started Silvie. "We were..."

"We were looking for some brochures for my dad," Adam cut in. "He loves anything that has to do with history."

"I see," said Ms. Crabtree."

"They didn't cause any trouble, but they shouldn't be wandering around without an adult," said Captain Leckal.

"Of course they shouldn't!" said Ms. Crabtree. "Thank you, Captain. It's time for us to pack up and get back to our bus. You two just missed lunch, and you'll be missing your afternoon recess, too!"

"Sorry kids," said Captain Leckal, sounding sincere. She turned and strode across the lawn.

Silvie watched Captain Leckal walk away.

"Gather your lunch trash and line up," said Ms. Crabtree.

Loud groans emanated from the class. Silvie looked across the grassy hill. Some groups were already moving toward the line of yellow school buses. A few others were still eating.

"I'm counting heads to make sure we're all here," said Ms. Crabtree, glaring at Silvie and Adam. When she had counted 28 children, Ms. Crabtree led them toward their bus on Sherman Street. It was easy to spot Curly's bald head where he sat on the bus steps. When Curly saw them approaching he stuffed the rest of whatever he was eating into his mouth.

By the time they reached the bus Curly was barking orders. "You know the rules. They haven't changed since this morning. Two to a seat; same pairs as on the way here!"

Silvie plopped into her seat next to Adam. The bus hummed with the noise of happy kids as Curly revved the engine, then slowly pulled away from the curb.

"What are you thinking, Blake?" asked Adam.

Silvie was thinking about Revi, her father, the two stolen paintings and the fact that her skin felt electric.

She decided to confide in Adam. "Revi said something about more secrets and the key."

"That's wild!" said Adam. "Do you think you can figure out the other secrets?"

Silvie swallowed before she spoke. "I don't know, Adam; but how did Revi know I have a key?"

Chapter 18

The bus turned onto 14th Avenue and headed east toward Dora Moore School.

"Maybe Revi knew you had a key because she saw us get off the elevator the first time we rode it," said Adam. "Maybe she knows you need a key to make it work, so she figures you have one."

"You're probably right," said Silvie, sounding more confident than she felt. She couldn't shake the strange feeling that Revi knew her father. And what did he have to do with the first stolen portrait of Lincoln? She wondered what else Revi knew.

"Of course Revi could be a ghost. That's why she knows about the key," suggested Adam.

"Now don't start that again!" said Silvie. "Maybe she stands behind the wall where the governor's painting hangs and spies on people through the eye holes."

"Maybe," said Adam.

The bus passed Grant Street, turned left onto Logan, rolled one block, and then made a right on Colfax Avenue.

Silvie got the newspaper word scramble out of her pocket. It would get her mind off of the things that had just happened. She read through the unscrambled words. They were planets, water, earth, and ghosts. She studied the circled letters in each word. There was A and N from planets, W and R from water, E from earth, and the two S's from ghosts. She reread the final riddle. It said, If you look you'll find the _ _ _ _ _ _ _ you seek.

"I've heard this riddle before," said Silvie.

"Where?" asked Adam.

"At the Capitol. Let me look through my notes," said Silvie. She found the section in her notebook on the water murals. There was the name, Nell Fishbone and the line, "If you look you'll find the answers you seek."

"ANWRESS, unscrambled spells ANSWERS!" said Silvie. "It's what Nell said to me when we were in the rotunda."

"Maybe she's a ghost, too," said Adam.

"Naw, I think she finished the word puzzle in the newspaper this morning before she came to work. That's how she knew the riddle and then told it to me," said Silvie.

"Maybe," said Adam.

Working the puzzle helped to calm Silvie's nerves on the ride back to school. In her mind she went over what she would tell the police as soon as she could get to a phone. She folded her word puzzle and put it back into her pocket. Her fingers grazed the metal key. "What other secrets are there?" she wondered.

Adam nudged Silvie. "Look, there's a group of homeless people heading toward Speer Boulevard. They probably live at the campsite we found."

"Let's hope they leave it untouched until I can make an anonymous phone call," said Silvie.

The bus bounced eastward along Colfax Avenue. They passed a pay phone hanging on the brick wall outside of Smiley's Laundromat. Silvie wished she could jump off the bus right there and make her call.

"Don't worry, Blake. Even if they move the painting, they can't travel very fast. They're pushing shopping carts, remember?" said Adam.

"You're probably right. I'll just feel better after I call the police," said Silvie.

The bus hit every stop light along the way, making the ride back as long as possible.

"Is it my imagination or is this taking forever?" asked Silvie.

"What's the rush? Crabtree will punish us when we get back. Let's enjoy our freedom while we have it," suggested Adam.

Silvie had never been punished at school before. Surprisingly, she wasn't panicked. She was much more concerned about calling the police and the things Revi had told her. Her mind was filled with an old elevator, a silver key, an unknown father, and secrets, secrets, secrets.

Chapter 19

The bus turned right on Corona Street. Silvie watched brick apartment buildings and houses go by. They headed south to 9th Avenue and turned left. Curly stopped in front of the historic castle-like school building.

"Here you are kids; home sweet home," said Curly.

Ms. Crabtree made her way to the front of the bus. "Follow me, class."

Silvie and Adam hopped off the bus. Josh came up behind them.

"It's too bad you two will miss afternoon recess," he said.

Adam nodded. Silvie felt sorrier for him than for herself. She didn't care about recess much, anyway.

Inside the classroom everyone took their seats.

"We have fifteen minutes before recess. You can all read except for Silvie and Adam," said Ms. Crabtree. "Come forward, you two."

Silvie and Adam walked to the front of the class.

"Do you think it's safe for children to walk away from their class during field trips?" inquired Ms. Crabtree.

"No," said Adam and Silvie in unison.

"We didn't mean to break the rules, Ms. Crabtree," said Silvie.

"Well, you did break them, twice. That's the reason you two will spend your recess writing about why it's important to follow school rules. I want 300 words apiece, so you'd better get started now," said Ms. Crabtree.

Silvie thought Adam looked a bit ill. She was glad when she saw him make a face at Josh on the way back to their seats.

Silvie took out paper and pencil and wrote, "It is very important to follow our school rules because they keep us safe, polite, and help us to learn." She stopped. Silvie counted the words in her sentence. There were twenty words. If I write this sentence fourteen more times I'll have 300 words, she thought.

"Class is dismissed for recess," said Ms. Crabtree.

"Sorry," Silvie mouthed to Adam.

"It's okay," he mouthed back.

Silvie rewrote her sentence over and over. Since she didn't have to think about what she was writing she thought about calling the police. School would be out in less than an hour.

Silvie finished her last sentence as the rest of the class returned from recess. Maggie and Brittney looked like they felt sad for her. She didn't like their pity, but she knew they were trying to be nice.

Adam finished writing and looked at Silvie. They walked to Ms. Crabtree's desk, and handed in their papers. Ms. Crabtree glanced at their writing. She must have been satisfied that the papers were long enough because she set them on top of a pile on her desk and motioned for Adam and Silvie to go to their seats.

"Let's clean out our desks before we go on spring break," said Ms. Crabtree. "If you finish early you can begin your reports on something in Colorado history you learned about on our field trip. Your papers are due on the Monday after break."

The classroom was a flurry of activity. Before Silvie knew it, the time passed. The fifth graders packed their backpacks and lined up. The bell rang, and children flooded out of Dora Moore School.

Silvie crossed 9th Avenue and noticed Adam at her side.

"I'm coming with you to make the call," he said.

"Let's walk to Colfax," said Silvie.

"Why not the grocery store across from school?" asked Adam.

"It won't be far enough away. Colfax is busy and there are a lot of pay phones," answered Silvie.

"Good thinking, Blake," said Adam.

They ran the whole six blocks toward Colfax together. Silvie stopped at the first pay phone she saw. She felt in her pocket. There was the folded puzzle and the key but no money.

"Can I borrow a quarter? I gave away all my change this morning," said Silvie.

"Sure," said Adam. He reached into his pocket and handed Silvie the coin.

"Wait a minute before you dial," said Adam. He jammed his hand into his pocket again and pulled out a scrap of paper. "It has my phone number on it in case you need to reach me over break," he said. "After you call the police we should split up and go home. People in the movies always split up."

"I agree," said Silvie. She took his phone number and put it in her pocket. Silvie dropped the quarter into the pay phone coin slot and dialed 9-1-1. When someone answered she said, "The stolen Lincoln painting from the state Capitol is under the viaduct near Speer Boulevard and 14th."

"I need your name and address, please," said the voice.

Silvie hung up the phone. "Let's get out of here," she said.

"See ya," said Adam. He turned and trotted west down Colfax.

Silvie sprinted two blocks east. She knew that the police would trace the call to the pay phone. Four lanes of cars whizzed by. The sidewalk crawled with people on both sides. Anyone could have made the call, but Silvie wanted distance from the pay phone by the time the police got there to check it.

Silvie stopped at a red light on the corner. A siren blared. She saw flashing red and blue lights. A police car pulled up to the corner where she stood and screeched to a stop.

Chapter 20

Watching from the second-hand book store doorway, Dwayne Beasley was sure he recognized the school girl from this morning at the pay phone on Colfax Avenue. He was walking back to the campsite after a profitable day of begging. He had counted $15.65 before he decided to call it quits. That was enough to pick up something to eat if he couldn't find any free food, and more importantly to him, something to drink.

Dwayne had seen the girl say a few words into the receiver and then hang up. She was standing there with a boy, but he took off in the opposite direction. Dwayne saw the girl walk in a hurry down Colfax, but she didn't see him.

Dwayne heard sirens. Suddenly, a police car came out of nowhere and stopped next to the girl. Dwayne thought he saw her jump. Then he saw a lady in the crosswalk pushing a baby stroller. After the woman and the baby made it safely across the street, the police car drove up onto the sidewalk and parked at the pay phone where the girl had made a call.

What in the world are they looking for, Dwayne wondered. He could tell the police that a school girl made a call from that phone a few minutes earlier, but he wasn't the type to talk to the police. Besides, that girl had given him some change this morning.

Dwayne then decided something must have happened at that spot right before the girl got there. She was lucky she missed the trouble beforehand and then the police visit afterward. She must be a very lucky kid, thought Dwayne. Somebody must be watching over a kid like that.

The police officers got out and checked the pay phone. There was nothing there to see. They got back into their car, gunned the motor, backed up, and headed west on Colfax Avenue.

Dwayne shielded his eyes from the sun and looked down the street for the school girl. He couldn't see her anymore.

Yes, he thought, somebody's looking out for that girl.

Chapter 21

Silvie stared straight ahead, avoiding the police car. She held her breath. All the cars were at a standstill. Then Silvie noticed a woman pushing a baby stroller through the crosswalk at the intersection. After they were safely on the sidewalk, the police car turned a half-circle around the stopped traffic and headed back in the direction of the pay phone.

Cars started moving again. Silvie started breathing again. The light turned green and she crossed the street. She walked as fast as she could without running. She didn't want to draw attention to herself. She didn't slow her pace until she was on her own front porch.

Breathless, Silvie burst through the door. Millie greeted her as always with unblinking green eyes. Silvie buried her face in the tabby's warm fluff. After she rubbed Millie's head, Silvie snacked on celery, peanut butter and an apple. She was hungry from a full day and from missing lunch.

She noticed a note from Gramps taped to the refrigerator.

"Silvie, I went to the post office and grocery store. I'll be home for dinner. Love, Gramps."

Silvie stared at the note. The house seemed empty without her grandfather now that Mama and Gram were gone. She had so much to tell Gramps about the Capitol, and the tunnel, and the stolen painting, and the police call, and Revi.

What a strange day this had been. Revi's words haunted her. Silvie wanted to talk to someone. She climbed the stairs to the second floor. She didn't usually go into Gramp's bedroom but Gram's photograph on the dresser pulled her into the room.

"What's going on, Gram?" Silvie said to the photo. "What are the secrets that Revi was talking about?"

Silvie ached for her grandmother so much that she picked up the picture and hugged it to herself. Her fingers grazed a loose object in back of the frame. She turned it over and revealed a folded piece of paper tucked between the frame and the photo. She pulled it out and unfolded the aged paper carefully so it wouldn't tear.

Silvie read the words printed in ink:

To my darling granddaughter, Kate, on her wedding day, I wish you all the good things life has to offer as you begin your marriage. You have been a wonderful granddaughter and daughter to me. Your mother, Nettie, would be proud of you if she were here today. I will tell you the same thing my mother told me when I was very young, before she got sick. A mother's love lives forever in your heart. Remember this always. It will comfort you.

With love, Your grandmother, Josie

Gram's grandmother was named Josie, thought Silvie. Revi's daughter was also named Josie, and she called me that name today. Revi is too young to have known Gram's grandmother, Josie, but maybe Revi knew Gram, and Gram told her about Josie.

Something about the message in the letter seemed familiar to Silvie.

"I'll return your grandmother's letter to you later, Gram. I promise," said Silvie, putting the photograph back on her grandparents' dresser.

She ran downstairs and found her notebook from the field trip. She flipped through the pages until she found Revi's name. There it was. Revi had told her the same words about a mother's love living forever inside your heart.

"This whole thing is getting weirder by the minute!" said Silvie to Millie.

The cat tilted her head and blinked at Silvie as if she understood.

Silvie continued going through her notebook. She stopped on a page. There was Amy R. Cashe. Silvie remembered how she had pointed out the dancer in the marble wall. Then when Silvie tried to find the picture again she couldn't.

She spotted Nell Fishbone's name in her notes. It was there next to "If you look you'll find the answers you seek." Nell must be a word unscrambler like me to have gotten today's riddle from the newspaper, thought Silvie. It's almost like Amy and Nell were trying to tell me something,

Out of habit, or curiosity, or on a hunch, she rewrote Nell Fishbone in a larger space on the page. She began playing with the name. "What if your name were Nell Bonefish?" she asked. "How about Ellen Nobfish?" That one made Silvie laugh. "I could take the H and make it Hellen. Actually, Helen has only one L, so how's Helen Lonfibs?" Silvie froze. She had passed Bonfils theater on Colfax Avenue enough times to recognize that she had all of the letters in Lonfibs to spell Bonfils. She remembered that Helen Bonfils was one of the women on the tapestry at the Capitol. Nell Fishbone could be rearranged to spell Helen Bonfils!

Chapter 22

Silvie stared at the unscrambled name. Her head tingled like every hair was standing on end. She reached down and ruffled Millie's fur. Silvie felt some comfort, but she wanted to talk to someone who could talk back to her. She fumbled through her pocket until she found the torn scrap of paper. She picked up the phone and dialed the number Adam had scribbled for her.

After the third ring she heard his familiar voice. "Hullo."

"It's Silvie," she said.

"Hey, you made it home okay?" he asked.

"Yeah. Adam, I'm working on some clues here."

"We already found the missing painting. What are these clues about?" asked Adam.

"Get paper and something to write with, and you'll see."

"I was going to meet the guys for a soccer game, but this sounds more interesting," said Adam. Silvie heard silence and then shuffling in the distance. Soon Adam said, "I got it."

"Good. Now write NELL FISHBONE is HELEN BONFILS."

"Who is Nell Fishbone?"

"She was one of the guides at the Capitol. She talked to us in the rotunda."

"Oh yeah, I remember her. So you think her name is a word scramble for the theater lady?" asked Adam.

"That's the way it looks," said Silvie.

"It's probably just a coincidence, Blake."

"Maybe it is, but maybe it's not. That's why I called you. I need your help to figure out a few more names."

"Why do you need my help? You're better at unscrambling words than I am."

"You started to get the hang of it on the bus. Besides, I want you to talk to me while I work on these names. It's creeping me out, and Gramps isn't home now."

"Okay. Let's do a scramble and see if you're on to something here.

Silvie looked through her notes. "Write down AMY R. CASHE. Do you see anything?"

"How about RAMY SHACE?" asked Adam.

"That doesn't mean anything to me, but RAMY has the same letters as MARY," said Silvie.

"Do we know any MARY's?" asked Adam.

"Hang on," said Silvie. She looked through her notes from the field trip. "I think I have it. Remember when Greta Rae told us about the woman on the tapestry who wrote the play called Harvey? The author was MARY COYLE CHASE. Her mouth felt dry. "AMY R. CASHE is MARY CHASE."

"Wow! Both names are women from the tapestry," said Adam. "This is weird. Have you looked at Greta Rae's name yet?"

"Let's do it next," said Silvie. She found Greta Rae's full name in the front of her notes. "Write GRETA RAE M. DRAWCROF."

"RAE is EAR spelled backwards," said Adam.

Silvie smiled. "You're right. Keep going," she said studying the letters.

"GRETA is GREAT unscrambled," offered Adam.

"Uh-huh," said Silvie working with the letters. "If you start with her middle initial M and put both words together you can spell MARGARET."

"I've got this one. I remember the rose lady. DRAWCROF can be CRAWFORD. GRETA RAE is MARGARET CRAWFORD," said Adam.

"No wonder she knew so much about that long wagon ride to bring her roses to Colorado," said Silvie.

"I told you that place was full of ghosts!" said Adam.

Silvie searched her brain for a logical explanation. Suddenly she found one. "I don't think they're ghosts, Adam."

"Well, what are they then?" he asked.

"I think they are guides who use these scrambled names when they work at the Capitol," said Silvie.

"You could be right, but why don't they just use the names of the historic women instead of scrambling them? Most tourists and kids would never figure these out," said Adam.

"Maybe it's a game they do for fun. It makes their job more interesting," suggested Silvie.

"Hey, how about that security guard who caught us in the basement? What was her name?" asked Adam.

Silvie flipped pages in her notebook until she found it. Even though there was a reasonable explanation for all of this, her skin felt crawly. "Write CAPTAIN JEN LECKAL," she said.

"What was that lady's name with the gun on the tapestry? Captain somebody," said Adam.

"CAPTAIN ELLEN JACK," Silvie replied. "The letters for ELLEN JACK are all here in JEN LECKAL."

"So it's not just the guides who have scrambled names. How about your friend?"

"What friend?"

"You know, the brass polisher."

"You mean Revi? Write down REVI ESHELLS."

"How about SHELLI REEVS?"

"Not bad." said Silvie, "But she isn't on the tapestry."

"You're right. The only other names I remember are the ELITCHES lady and the dancer, somebody HEELS."

"That's it!"

"What's it?" asked Adam.

"It's the dancer. It spells SILVER HEELS."

"These really aren't clues to anything, Silvie. We just have a bunch of workers who like to use scrambled up historic names at work."

"So you're giving up on your ghost idea?" asked Silvie.

"Are you?" asked Adam.

"You know I don't believe in ghosts, but something has me stumped. Revi knew I had the key to the elevator without me telling her."

"So what? She saw us get out of the thing, remember?"

"There's more," said Silvie.

"What?' asked Adam.

"She said that the key opens more secrets," said Silvie.

"Oooooo, that sounds ghost-like to me. My dad says ghosts hang around if they have unfinished business or if they need to get a message to somebody."

"That's crazy!"

"It sounds like Revi or Silver Heels had a message for you, Blake."

"No way! This is the first I ever knew somebody named Silver Heels even existed. Why would she want to talk to me?" asked Silvie.

"She was a dancer. You want to be a dancer."

"Revi didn't offer me dance lessons," said Silvie. She meant it as a joke.

"No she didn't, but she was following us around, and she did talk with you about the key. Did she say anything else?"

"She said I could find the stolen painting."

"Revi was right. You found it."

"No Adam; she said to ask my father about the first painting of Lincoln that was stolen in 1994."

"That's spooky! Maybe she knows your father," suggested Adam.

"Maybe she did know him, but my father took off before I was born. I've never met him."

"Whoa! Are you sure you don't know anything about Silver Heels?"

"I'm sure. Why do you ask?"

"Because Silver Heels seems to know a lot about you!"

There was static on the phone. When it cleared Silvie said, "I see what you mean. Revi, the woman at the Capitol who is using Silver Heels' name does seem to know a bit about me," said Silvie.

"Do you have any history books at your house, Blake?" asked Adam.

"Not really. We have the Internet."

"We have books and the Internet too, but there are newspaper articles and stuff like that at the library," said Adam.

"How do you know about this?"

"My dad makes me go along sometimes when he does research. I didn't think I would ever want to use it myself."

Silvie looked at the clock. Dinner at the Blake house was usually at six. Gramps probably wouldn't be home until right before then.

"You're right, Adam. I'm taking the bus downtown to the Denver Public Library. I'm going to find out everything I can about Silver Heels and what it is she has to do with me!"

Chapter 23

"I'm coming with you," said Adam.

"I didn't think you liked history," said Silvie.

"I don't like history," he said. "But I like mysteries and ghosts, and I think you're right in the middle of both of them!"

"The bus stop is near my house. I can be at the library in twenty minutes."

"I'll see you there. And Silvie, don't tell the guys at school I went with you to the library."

"I won't tell. I'm good at secrets."

She heard the dial tone. She wrote a message to Gramps on the bottom of his note to her. "Dear Gramps, I went to the library downtown to do research for a school project. I'll be home by dinner time. Love, S."

Silvie grabbed her notebook and a pen. She got some change out of the top kitchen drawer. Millie looked at her with curious emerald eyes.

"I know what you want," said Silvie. "We'll play after dinner. I promise."

She scratched her kitty under her collar and kissed the top of her head. Silvie glanced at the clock; it flashed 3:55. She bolted out of the front door. She could make it to the corner in time for the four o'clock bus.

Silvie jogged to the end of her block. She saw the huge silver RTD bus, Number 6, heading toward her. It glided to where she stood, and she heard the brakes work against the wheels with a loud 'whoosh' as it stopped. The doors opened, and she climbed the steps onto the public bus. She dropped two quarters into the metal box near the driver. The bus jerked forward. The ballet dancer inside of her did a graceful hop to keep her balance before landing on an open seat.

Silvie watched her city whiz by through the bus window. Sitting still brought the reality of today's events into focus.

Adam and I found the stolen painting, she thought. We solved one mystery only to open up another one. Now, I'm trying to find out why Revi is using

Silver Heels' name, and what she was trying to tell me about my father. If only Gram were still alive. She could explain how she knew Revi and why Revi knows about our family.

Silvie opened her notebook to a blank page. She wrote her own name. Under it she wrote Mama's name, Lizzie. Underneath that she wrote Gram's name, Kate. Under Kate she wrote Nettie, and under Nettie she wrote Josie. She took Gram's letter from the photograph out of her pocket. She reread the line that said, "I will tell you the same thing my mother told me when I was very young before she got sick." Under Josie's name on her list Silvie wrote, "Sick mother???"

The bus stopped at a traffic light. Silvie looked up, and noted that they were at the corner of Broadway and 13th Avenue. The multicolored Denver Public Library filled the whole front window of the bus.

Silvie's attention was drawn to the street beyond the library where police cars and people were gathered. She figured they were all at the spot where she and Adam had found the painting. I'm glad I'm not down there now, she thought.

The light turned green and the bus pulled forward. It stopped at the corner near the main entrance of the gigantic library. Silvie spotted Adam as she hopped off the bus.

"Did you see the commotion under the viaduct?" asked Adam.

"I saw. I'm sure they have the painting by now," said Silvie.

"Stolen Painting Case closed. Now, Detective Blake, shall we move onto the Capitol Guide and Brass Polisher Case?" asked Adam mimicking an English accent.

"Indeed we shall," chimed in Silvie, copying the accent.

They walked into the library and strode across the immense open corridor to the elevators. Inside, Adam pushed the button for the fifth floor. The sign next to it read, "Western History/Genealogy Department."

"Silver Heels, here we come," said Adam.

Silvie shook her head and laughed as they ascended. The elevator stopped and the two junior detectives stepped out onto the fifth floor.

Silvie saw bronze statues of cowboys on horses and black and white paintings of miners.

"It's to the left," said Adam, gesturing.

They walked through more large doors into a huge room with microfiche machines, computers, and a wall of tiny drawers.

"They keep newspaper articles from over one hundred years ago on the microfiche films in those drawers," said Adam.

Silvie nodded.

"Can I help you kids?" asked a thin man with glasses behind the circular wooden counter.

"We're looking for information on Silver Heels," said Silvie.

"Put her name into the computer over there and it will tell you which articles you can find her in," said the man.

"Thanks," said Silvie.

She settled in a seat in front of a computer screen and typed in SILVER HEELS.

The monitor clicked a few times and then the screen lit up with a list of articles:

Silver Heels Lives in Mining Camp Legends, Rocky Mountain News, Oct. 6, 1938.

Silver Heels, Mystery Dancer of Boom Colorado Mining Camp, is Recalled by Old Prospector, Montrose Daily Press, Oct. 11, 1938.

Old Gold Miner Recounts Story of Mystery Girl "Silver Heels" Who Danced Always With Mask, The Pueblo Star, Dec. 12, 1938.

Silver Heels--Dance Hall Queen and Angel of Mercy, Colorado Springs Gazette, Jan. 3, 1954.

Legend of Silver Heels, Pueblo Star Journal, May 17, 1959.

"What do you think?" asked Adam.

"Let's look at the oldest articles. They'll be the most accurate," suggested Silvie.

"Good idea," he agreed.

Silvie wrote down the newspaper names and dates in her notebook. She and Adam headed for the cabinets with hundreds of drawers. Before long they had three rolls of film with articles dating back to the 1930s in hand. They chose a microfiche machine and sat down.

"I've seen my dad do this a million times," said Adam, as he threaded the film into the machine. He scrolled until the article on Silver Heels appeared. He watched out of the 5th floor window while Silvie read one article after another. When she finally sat back he asked, "What do they say?"

"They say that a young, beautiful dancer arrived in the mining town of Buckskin Joe wearing fancy silver heeled shoes. The town was named after a guy called Bill Buck. Some people think the dancer was from the south and left during the Civil War. She was the finest dancer and the miners respected her. She had long dark hair and always wore a veil over her face. She became Bill Buck's girl. He eventually got her to take off her veil. She was gorgeous. She always danced in her silver heels. No one knew her by any name other than Silver Heels. One day a sheepherder came through Buckskin Joe selling sheep. He died of smallpox a few days later. The disease he carried started to spread. Most of the women left, but Silver Heels was brave. She stayed to help the sick."

Silvie paused for a moment. This part of the story reminded her of Gram and Mama. Her chest felt heavy, but she continued.

"Silver Heels nursed man after man until most of them died. Bill Buck got pneumonia and died in Silver Heels' arms. Eventually Silver Heels got sick too. After she recovered she got on her best clothes and looked in the mirror. She saw in her reflection that her face was covered with pockmark scars from the disease."

She touched her own cheeks for a moment.

"I know how she must have felt," said Silvie, softly. "Silver Heels disappeared after that. People reported often seeing a woman with a black veil on her face putting flowers on the graves of dead miners, but they never saw Silver Heels again. One day some miners found gold in a mountain near Fairplay. They said the mountain was like Silver Heels because it was beautiful to look at, and it had a heart of gold. They named the mountain after her," finished Silvie.

"It sounds like she was a real hero," said Adam.

"I guess that's why Revi wanted to use her name at work at the Capitol," said Silvie.

"Yeah. It could be that," said Adam. "but there could be another explanation. There's something I have to tell you."

Chapter 24

"Do you know something about Silver Heels that isn't in these articles?" asked Silvie.

"Not exactly; but something else could be going on here," said Adam. "Look Blake, my dad read a book about this plane that crashed in 1972. I think he said it was Eastern Airlines Flight 401, or 407, or something like that. A bunch of people died including the pilot. Anyway, a few months later some guy is on a flight and starts talking with a passenger in uniform who's sitting alone in first class. Pretty soon he figures out he's talking to the pilot of the crashed plane. Then the pilot vanishes into thin air!"

"No way! You're making this up, Westin!" said Silvie.

"Let me finish, Blake. After that, a couple of guys from the pilot's crew saw him sitting in a staff room at the J. F. Kennedy Airport in New York. The pilot talked to them and then disappeared."

"This cannot be true!" said Silvie.

"Yeah well, the other pilots were so freaked out they had to cancel their flight."

"You're freaking me out right now."

"All I know is that a bunch of people saw the pilot's ghost. He started appearing on different flights. Other people saw the ghost of the flight engineer, too. One time he warned some workers of a fire that was about to happen. Sure enough, it did. Both the pilot and engineer kept on showing up. Somebody finally figured out that the ghosts were appearing on all the planes that had used the spare parts from their crashed airplane," explained Adam.

Silvie shivered. "This is giving me the creeps."

"I guess it gave the big boss of Eastern Airlines the creeps, too," said Adam. "He ordered all of the parts from the crash to be removed from the planes. As soon as all the parts were removed, the ghosts disappeared. It was as if they came back to do a job. So maybe this is like Revi."

"How is this like Revi?" asked Silvie.

"Maybe she really is Silver Heels. Maybe she's here doing a job and she needs your help. Maybe she knows your family or likes you because you have scars on your face like her. Maybe she wants you to get the painting back or something like that," said Adam.

"I don't know, Westin. This is pretty farfetched," said Silvie. "I suppose you think that all those people with mixed up names are her ghost friends and they came back to help her."

"It does sound crazy, but I'm sure the people who saw the pilot and engineer thought it was crazy too. Anyhow, maybe Revi knew your grandma, or your mom, or your father. Maybe that's why she talked to you," said Adam. "Hey, do the articles say anything about Silver Heels having any kids or anything?"

Silvie turned the crank and rolled a film. "Not really. This one article says that Bill Buck left her his fortune before he died." She scanned the print on the screen in front of her. "Wait, this article says that a woman named Aunt Martha nursed Silver Heels back to health. She was seen caring for an infant girl. It says that Aunt Martha, a priest, and a lawyer were the only ones who saw Silver Heels after she disappeared from public."

"That must have been her baby that Aunt Martha took care of. I wonder what happened to her kid?" asked Adam.

"Maybe Aunt Martha raised her," suggested Silvie.

"She probably had to raise her since Silver Heels was so sick, and then didn't want anyone to see her," said Adam.

"That must have been hard to have such a sick mother," said Silvie.

"Yeah."

Silvie barely heard him. She was already flipping through the pages of her notebook. Finally she found the list of names she was looking for. Her eyes focused on the spot after Josie's name where earlier she had written, "Sick mother???"

Chapter 25

It was almost four by the time Dwayne Beasley walked all the way down Colfax Avenue to the campsite. He was looking forward to hanging out around the bonfire they made each night inside of an old metal trash can.

Dwayne shifted the bottle wrapped in a brown paper bag inside his coat pocket. Whiskey prices were the lowest at Argonaut on Colfax and Washington Street. He had been a regular customer for a couple of weeks. Dwayne had a sip outside the store. He had another sip near the Cathedral at Colfax and Logan Street. He had a third sip after he crossed Broadway.

Dwayne was feeling very relaxed until he saw the police cars at the campsite. His heart rate increased and blood pounded into his temples. Police officers were talking to people with shopping carts, people dressed in ragged clothes; people without homes like Dwayne Beasley.

Dwayne stopped walking. He leaned up against a brick building and watched. He saw them put a rectangular object into one of the police cars. He knew it was the portrait of President Lincoln he had stolen from the Capitol.

That's okay with me, thought Dwayne. That painting didn't do me any good. Then he saw them put a few of the wanderers into the police cars including her. He watched her bend down and a policewoman help her get into a squad car. Maybe you'll have a warm place to sleep tonight and a hot meal anyway, he thought.

Dwayne had seen enough. He tightened his grip on the neck of the bottle in his pocket. He turned and headed back up Colfax Avenue; back the way he had come. He was used to leaving. This campsite was no different than the hundreds he'd left before.

Chapter 26

"Are you okay?" asked Adam from his perch at the fifth-floor library window. "All the color fell out of your face."

"Yeah, I think I've been looking at the microfiche screen too long," Silvie said, trying to mask her feelings. "It makes me feel woozy, when I watch the articles spin by."

"If that's all it takes to make you woozy, you definitely wouldn't like Tower of Doom and the other rides at Elitches," said Adam.

"You're right; I probably wouldn't like them," said Silvie. She glanced at the clock on the library wall. "It's after five. We'd better get going. I left a note for Gramps saying I'd be home by dinner."

Adam looked at Silvie for a moment. "I heard about your mom disappearing in Iraq last summer. It's gotta be tough not having a dad and then no mom either."

Adam's words took Silvie by surprise. "It's pretty hard sometimes," she replied, blinking away the tears that threatened to fill her eyes. "But I have Gramps."

"I think it would be cool to live with my grandfather. He's a lot more fun than my dad," said Adam. "Is Gramps a pretty good guy?"

"Uh-huh," said Silvie. A smile spread across her face. "You'd like him. You can come over and meet him sometime if you want."

"Okay. We'd better put the films away," said Adam.

They returned the films to their proper drawers and made their way to the elevators.

"So Blake, what are you thinking about Revi and Silver Heels?" asked Adam.

"I still think that all the guides and other museum workers pick historical Colorado names to use while they're at work. Maybe Revi likes dancers, or maybe it was one of the tapestry women's names that nobody else had taken," said Silvie.

"That sounds logical," said Adam, "but how does Revi know about your dad? Also, what was she trying to say about the first stolen painting?"

The elevator stopped on the main floor of the library. As she and Adam stepped out, Silvie dug in her pants and pulled out the silver key.

"Revi said this key opens more secrets and to ask my dad about the first portrait of Lincoln that was stolen," said Silvie.

"I don't know how you're going to find out whatever else that key opens, and it's impossible to ask your dad anything. I know you're good at figuring out puzzles, but I don't see what you can do with these last two pieces," said Adam.

I may have three pieces if 'sick mother' means anything, thought Silvie. "I don't know either. I'll work on it after dinner. If I get anything, I'll call you."

"You'd better call, Blake. If I don't hear from you by tomorrow I'm calling you. I'm too far into this to stop now," said Adam. "Do you really think we can find the first stolen portrait of Lincoln like Revi says?"

"I don't know. We found the one that was stolen yesterday. Maybe we can find the original one, too."

"Hey, if we find it maybe we'll get a reward. Maybe we'll be millionaires!"

They walked to the front lobby and out of the gigantic double doors.

"Maybe," said Silvie, "but I don't think so. It's unlikely that they would give us kids a bunch of money. Even so, if we do find it, and if there is a reward, what would you do with your half?"

"My half? Well, my dad would want me to do something boring like save it for college and law school, but I'd rather go to summer space camp for kids and blow the rest at Elitches or even Disneyland!" said Adam.

Silvie laughed and nodded. They walked in the brisk air toward the bus stop on Broadway.

"What would you do, Blake, if we got a reward and you were suddenly rich?" asked Adam.

Silvie thought for a moment. She had never taken the luxury of even considering being rich before. "I think I would have plastic surgery on my face to get rid of my scars, and then I would sign up for ballet lessons."

Adam stopped on the sidewalk and looked at her.

"Your scars aren't really that bad, you know," he said. "You should try out the ballet lessons, anyway."

"What good would lessons do me? My face makes me feel too self conscious," said Silvie.

"Couldn't you wear makeup or something?" asked Adam.

"I don't think makeup would cover my burns enough," said Silvie.

"Hey, the way you're always hiding your face and not dancing reminds me of Silver Heels. She did the same thing," said Adam.

"Yeah, I guess you're right," Silvie replied. "I can imagine how she felt after she got smallpox scars all over her face. She hid from everyone after that," Silvie halted at the bus stop. The sun hung in the western sky over the Rocky Mountains on its way to setting.

"Blake, maybe we'll find the original stolen portrait just like we found the second one, and maybe we'll get rich, and maybe you can get your scars fixed the way you like," said Adam, waiting at the bus stop with her.

Silvie faced him. "I'll study these clues and see what we have. We just might be able to find it, Westin. Maybe we'll even be detectives when we grow up."

"You could be right, Blake. Actually, don't you think it's kind of weird that a couple of fifth grade kids solved a crime that the police and a bunch of grown-ups couldn't solve?"

"Yeah, I see what you mean. It's almost like we were meant to find that painting. We got stuck together when Ms. Crabtree made us partners. Then we found the stolen Lincoln painting. Now we're working together on another case."

Silvie saw the Number 6 bus approaching.

"So you're saying this is all meant to be somehow?" asked Adam.

"Well, it is odd," said Silvie. "It's like fate, or destiny, or..."

"Or like a bunch of ghosts picked us to get their paintings back!" finished Adam.

"I didn't say that!" said Silvie.

The RTD bus rolled to a stop in front of them.

"No, you didn't say it, but it's possible," said Adam. "Think of the pilot ghost from that plane crash. If that's possible, this is possible, too!"

Silvie stepped onto the bus.

"It's possible only if you believe in ghosts, you wacko, Westin!" she teased.

"Maybe you don't have to believe in ghosts, Blake," said Adam, "as long as they believe in you!"

Chapter 27

The bus doors closed. Silvie made the cuckoo sign at Adam. He laughed and took off in the opposite direction.

Silvie dropped her quarters in the box and flopped into the first open seat.

She flipped through the pages of her notebook until she found the one she was looking for. She ran her finger down the list of names. Looking at the words *sick mother* made her feel strange, although anything referring to mother could make her feel uneasy.

Under the names Silvie, wrote, "First Lincoln portrait stolen 1994. Second Lincoln portrait stolen 2007." She added, "Colorado State Capitol, underground tunnels, silver elevator key, guides and workers with names of heroic women from the Women's Gold Tapestry."

The bus bumped along. Through the windows, Silvie saw a scruffy man walking on Colfax. In his left hand, he carried a brown bag, twisted at the top and shaped like a bottle. It was the man who had been begging at the corner of Josephine and Colfax this morning. The man looked into her window as the bus passed.

Even if he sees me, he probably doesn't remember me, thought Silvie. I remember him, though. I remember the other homeless people living under the viaduct where we found the stolen portrait, too. I wonder if the police have returned the painting to the Capitol yet.

The bus turned onto Silvie's street and slowed to a stop at the corner. She closed her notebook and jumped off. A few moments later, Silvie walked through the front door. The house smelled like Gramps' homemade chili.

"Silvie, is that you?" he called.

"I'm home, Gramps," she said, making a beeline for the kitchen. She fell into her grandfather's bear hug. He smelled like day-old aftershave and the chili he cooked. A portable T.V. on top of the fridge was tuned to a local news station.

"How was school and your field trip?" he asked.

"It was fun," Silvie replied. "I made friends with a boy named Adam. We've actually been in the same class for years, but today we started being friends."

"That's nice. I was just listening to the six o'clock news before you came in. It looks like they may have located that stolen Lincoln portrait," said Gramps.

"Really?" asked Silvie, acting surprised.

"Yes siree! They're going to have the story on after this commercial," said Gramps.

Silvie opened a kitchen drawer and pulled out two soup spoons and a couple of butter knives. She knew what was baking in the oven without even asking Gramps. Chili and cornbread was one of their set meals.

"Did you find what you were looking for at the library?" asked Gramps.

"Uh-huh. My friend Adam, showed me how to look up stuff in old newspaper articles," said Silvie.

"What were you researching? Wait," said Gramps, interrupting himself. "Here's the story on that stolen painting."

He reached up and adjusted the sound on the T.V. Silvie saw the familiar scene under the viaduct appear as the announcer told how a tip had been phoned in to the police. They responded in record time and recovered the portrait of Lincoln in a camp set up by some homeless people.

"Go figure," said Gramps, shaking his head. "What would a bunch of homeless folks want with a painting of Honest Abe?"

"I don't know," said Silvie.

The announcer went on to say that the police had arrested several of the vagrant individuals, but they thought it was possible that the painting could have been left by someone else. They were still looking for other suspects.

Silvie bent down and poked her head deep into a bottom cupboard. She was looking for Millie's favorite cat food. It was the least she could do since she'd been out all day.

"It couldn't be!" she heard Gramps exclaim.

"Ah, there it is," Silvie said, pulling the small can of chicken tidbits out from under the stack. She stood up. The picture on the T.V. was back on the newscasters and off the viaduct scene. She felt relieved. She couldn't tell

Gramps the truth about the painting and being there today. It felt the same as lying, and Silvie had no intentions of getting used to the feeling. "It couldn't be what?" she asked.

Gramps kept his back to her and blew his nose loudly on his handkerchief. He cleared his throat.

"What is it, Gramps?" Silvie said.

"Oh it's nothing. I just got a whisker up my nose. Let's dish out that chili and eat!" he said.

Silvie was famished. Gramps opened the oven door and pulled out a pan of cornbread.

They sat at the kitchen table and dug in. The chili warmed Silvie's insides. She spread butter on a piece of steaming cornbread and watched it turn to golden liquid.

"Tell me about your field trip," said Gramps.

"It was the usual history stuff about the Capitol, like you'd expect. The guides were pretty weird, though. They took on names of people in Colorado's history," said Silvie.

"They've always done that," said Gramps. "I think I had a tour with Molly Brown one time when Gram and I visited the Capitol."

"Really?" asked Silvie in disbelief. She suddenly felt her clues about Revi and Silver Heels were way off the mark. "Were the guides' names all scrambled up?" asked Silvie.

"Scrambled up? Of course not! What good would that do? Nobody would ever figure them out!" said Gramps.

"Yeah, that was a silly question," said Silvie. She felt clever to have gotten the answer without exposing her suspicions. *What are my suspicions anyway?* she thought. *It still makes no sense to me that Revi knows me and my family.*

"Gramps, did you or Gram have any friends who worked at the Capitol?" asked Silvie.

"I didn't. Maybe Gram did, though. She had friends everywhere in this city. It seemed like she helped so many people, they were all connected in one way or another," said Gramps. "Why do you ask?"

"There was a worker there who thought she knew me," said Silvie.

"That's odd. We really haven't known anyone to work at the Capitol. Not since your father..." Gramps stopped.

"Not since my father what?" asked Silvie.

"Your father mopped floors at the Capitol for a short time. It was about the only real job he ever had. It didn't last long. He took off shortly after he quit that job," said Gramps.

"You, Gram and Mama never talked about him much," said Silvie.

"There wasn't much to talk about with the kind of man he was, Silvie," said Gramps. "You're better off without him."

Silvie picked up the empty bowls and carried them to the sink.

"You never told me what you were researching at the library," said Gramps.

"I was looking up information on one of the heroic women from the Women's Gold Tapestry," said Silvie, trying not to be too specific.

"If you like history, your Grandma had a box full of old photos and clothes that might interest you," said Gramps.

"Sure, I would like to see it," said Silvie.

"It looks like we're done with dinner. Follow me," said Gramps.

They walked up the stairs into the bedroom that Gramps and Gram had shared. Gramps shuffled around in the closet until he dragged out an old cardboard box.

"You can go through this stuff. I'll finish the dishes," said Gramps.

"Thanks," said Silvie.

Gramps left the room as Silvie opened the flaps of the old box. She blew a layer of dust off the top of some red material and pulled out an old-fashioned dress. It looked too ancient to have been worn by Gram.

Next was a photograph of a woman and a little girl. Silvie turned it over. The words, "Kate and Grandma Josie" were printed on the back. Silvie found a stiff corset with laces and an old stained baby blanket. Underneath it, she found half a silver heart-shaped locket. The initials BB were engraved in the inside.

Then, Silvie came upon one other item in the box; it was a woman's silver-heeled shoe.

Chapter 28

"Are you finding anything interesting?" called Gramps from downstairs.

"There's a bunch of old things in this box," said Silvie.

"Yeah, I know," said Gramps, coming up the steps. He walked back into the bedroom. "I almost pitched that box of junk after Gram passed, but then I couldn't bear to get rid of any of her things."

"I'm glad you saved this stuff," said Silvie. "Do you know anything about this silver-heeled shoe?" She tried to sound only mildly interested.

"I told Gram she should get rid of it since there's only one. What good is a shoe without its mate?" said Gramps.

Silvie noticed his eyes glistened with unspilled tears.

"That lonely old shoe is a little bit like your old Gramps," he said softly.

Silvie put her arms around him. They hugged in silence. Silvie felt sad thinking of Gram and Mama. The circle of Gramps' arms offered her some relief.

"You can have this stuff if you want it," said Gramps.

Glad to be distracted from missing the women who were no longer there, Silvie went over to the pile.

"Thanks, Gramps. Do you know anything about this half of a locket?" asked Silvie.

"Like I said, it's all from Gram's past. Maybe you can play dress-up with it unless you're too old by now," said Gramps. "I'm going downstairs."

He walked to the door and turned around.

"I know it's hard for you without your mama, but you have me to take care of you. I raised your mama and I can finish raising you too."

"I know Gramps. It'll be okay," said Silvie. She watched him disappear and heard his wide feet clunk down the wooden steps.

Silvie put everything back into the box. She placed the shoe and locket half on top of the pile. Her chest felt heavy as she looked at Gram's photo.

"Thanks for hanging on to this stuff, Gram," she said.

Silvie dragged the box into her bedroom. She pulled out her notebook and reread her list. At the bottom she added, "one silver-heeled shoe." Maybe, one of the women in her family history was a dancer like Silver Heels. Maybe, she danced with Silver Heels herself and knew her. And then, maybe Silver Heels gave her this shoe as a keepsake; or maybe Gram's great-grandmother took one of the shoes when Silver Heels died. Maybe, if Revi is a ghost like Adam thinks, she came to get her shoe back and got involved in the stolen portrait of Lincoln. Silvie smiled and shook her head at the thought. "Except, I don't believe in ghosts!"

Silvie went downstairs and found Gramps flipping channels between the evening news reports. He turned off the T.V. when he saw Silvie.

"Did you find any more treasures in that old stuff?" asked Gramps.

"Not really, just the things you saw," said Silvie. "Did Gram have anything else from her mother or grandmother?"

"That's it. Did you find the riddle in the shoe?"

"What riddle in the shoe?"

"There was a strip of paper in that old shoe with a riddle on it. Your Gram showed it to me years ago. We couldn't make heads or tails of it."

"Did anyone else see it?"

"Of course! Your Mama tried to help us figure it out. She even showed it to that no-good… to that father of yours, too."

"Did he figure it out?"

"Nope, come to think of it, I haven't seen it for years. I haven't seen it since he was hanging around here. He probably took it, or lost it."

"I wish I could have seen it. Do you remember it?" Silvie asked, hopefully.

"Not really," Gramps replied. "It didn't make sense. It said something about silver and a little babe. I remember that part, and something else about Honest Abe, and the Capitol."

Silvie's mind recorded silver, Capitol and Lincoln. Those things had all been a part of her day.

"It really doesn't make sense," said Silvie.

"That's what I told your Gram. Twenty-five years later, I said the same thing to your mama and your father," said Gramps. "Of course he was convinced that the riddle was the key to some kind of fortune. He was always looking for easy money."

"Did he try to find a fortune?"

"Your father always perked up when money was involved. I think he played around with the riddle for a while. Then he got bored with it like everything else. He worked at the Capitol for a short time, long enough to earn a few bucks. He painted for a short time, long enough to paint that portrait of your mama. He loved her for a short time, long enough to bring you into the world, and that was it," said Gramps.

"Is there anything else of his here?" Silvie felt more like a detective on a case than his granddaughter when she asked that question.

Gramps thought for a moment. "Your mama might have saved a picture of him somewhere to show you one day. She got rid of most of his things after he left. She didn't want the memory of him around here. He was always giving her little charms, and rabbits' feet for good luck. The luckiest thing he probably did was to get out of her life," said Gramps.

"Did she save any of the good luck charms or anything?" asked Silvie.

"I didn't think she did, but do you remember the day we took your mama to the airport when she left for Iraq?"

"Of course I do." Silvie's throat tightened.

"When I said good-bye to your mama and hugged her I noticed a chain around her neck under her collar in the back of her shirt. It was strange because she didn't wear jewelry. I've thought about it, especially since she disappeared. My mind wants to remember every detail of the last time I saw her."

"I know. I can see her so clearly, too."

"Well, I think she was wearing one of those good luck charms your father gave her around her neck on that chain."

Silvie wondered if Mama was wearing the other half of the locket she found in Gram's box. "Do you ever think she's still alive?" asked Silvie, afraid to hear Gramps' answer.

"Every day, Sweetie, I think she's alive every day; and then I look around here and I know she's gone."

"Sometimes it makes me feel better to hope. They never found her body after the explosion."

"In an explosion there's not much left; but sometimes, hoping makes us feel better."

"It's sad when people are gone. All you have are your memories and a bunch of leftovers."

"Our house is full of leftovers — Gram's leftovers, your mama's leftovers, and that leftover portrait of your mama, my Lizzie, that your father painted."

"If you didn't like my father so much, why did you hang the picture he painted right in the entryway of our house?" asked Silvie.

"I didn't hang it there; your father did on the night before he took off. For your mama's sake, I didn't have the heart to move it. It was like his good-bye note," said Gramps.

"He hung it there himself, and no one has touched it ever since?" asked Silvie.

"Right."

Silvie walked into the entryway. She flipped on the light and stared at the crude likeness of Mama in the painting. She reached up, and for the first time, lifted the portrait off of the two nails that held it on the wall.

The painting was surprisingly heavy. The huge hand-made wooden frame held a thick canvas. The wall behind the painting showed a dark rectangle the same size as the frame. Years of sunlight had faded the rest of the wall while her father's artwork sheltered this spot.

Silvie traced Mama's face with her finger. She felt a tear run all the way down her cheek. It hit the painting below Mama's left eye and ran down her painted face.

Silvie cleared her head. Did this painting hold secrets for her? She turned it over and carefully scanned the backside. She saw how her father had nailed the wood together at the corners, and then nailed a strip of brown leather across the tip of the triangular corners to reinforce them.

Silvie lifted the painting to hang it back up. Her eye caught something sticking out of the bottom right corner just above the leather strip. She eased it out of its hiding place and stared at the yellowed paper in her hands.

Chapter 29

Silvie read the words on the aged paper. They were written in riddle form.

It was early in the West
at the Capitol and 16th Honest Abe
Silver is the key three times
for a special little babe.

"Gramps, I found it!" Silvie exclaimed.

"You found what?" asked Gramps getting up and coming into the entry-way.

"Is this the riddle you told me about?" asked Silvie.

"Well, I'll be," Gramps replied. "It's the paper we found in that old shoe. Where was it?"

"It was stuck in back of this frame."

"Your father must have put it there."

"That's what I'm thinking, too."

"Well, you have it now. Maybe you can figure it out. Nobody else has been able to make much sense of it."

"You know I like puzzles. Is it okay if I take it up to my room and see what I can come up with?"

"Okay Sweetheart, I'll be using the phone."

Silvie hoisted the painting up onto her knee, and Gramps helped her lift it back on top of the nails. Her tear had dried on Mama's painted face leaving a shiny mark. She reached up and touched the spot. "I'll never get over losing you, Mama," she said softly.

Silvie took the steps two at a time and went into her room. She got out her notebook and propped up a couple of pillows at the head of her bed. She reread the clues she'd written after the section where she had unscrambled the names of the workers from the Capitol. She tore the sheet out of her spiral notebook. At the top of a fresh page she wrote: Clues. Underneath she wrote in order:

1. 1st stolen Lincoln portrait - 1994
2. 2nd stolen Lincoln portrait - 2007
3. Capitol workers with historical names
4. Silver elevator key and underground tunnels at Capitol
5. Found 2nd stolen Lincoln portrait
6. Revi says key and father are clues to 1st stolen painting
7. Revi called me Josie, her daughter's name
8. Gram's grandmother was named Josie

Silvie decided that she needed to list the women in her family in chronological order. She left a space and wrote:

Silvie-born 1997,

Mama Lizzie-born 1963,

Gram Kate-born1931,

great-grandmother Nettie-born about 1900,

great-great grandmother Josie-born about 1875,

great-great-great grandma (sick mother)-born about 1845,

She left another space and wrote: Gram's old stuff:

1. photo of Gram and Grandma Josie
2. half of silver locket with BB
3. one silver heeled shoe

On a fresh sheet she listed the main words in the riddle:

was early in the west

Capitol

16th

Honest Abe

silver is the key

little babe

Silvie picked up the phone to call Adam. She heard Gramps talking on the other end, "I will be there at nine o'clock tomorrow. Thanks."

"Sorry, Gramps!" she called.

He bounded up the stairs.

"Did you hear my conversation?" he asked.

"I just heard you say you're going somewhere at nine o'clock tomorrow," Silvie replied. "I apologize. I forgot you were using the phone."

"It's no problem. You can use it now. I'm finished," he said.

Silvie waited for the dial tone and then punched in Adam's number.

After three rings a man's voice answered, "Hello."

"Hello. Is Adam there please?" asked Silvie.

"Sure," the man said. "Adam, you have a call. It's a girl!"

Adam was on the phone in a moment. "Hi Blake, I figured it was you. You're the only girl who has my number." Then he yelled, "I've got it Dad; you can hang up, now."

There was a loud click.

"So, that was your dad, the lawyer?" asked Silvie.

"That was him," answered Adam.

"He sounds pretty nice."

"He's okay. So, what's up, Blake?"

"Weird things happened here tonight. My grandfather gave me some old stuff that belonged to my grandma."

"What was it?" asked Adam.

"It was mostly old clothes and a photo of Gram and her grandmother; but there was half of a silver locket with BB on it and one silver-heeled shoe."

"That's weird, especially since we spent the afternoon looking up the story on Silver Heels. Do you think it's her shoe?"

"I don't know. How would Gram have her shoe? The strange thing is I don't know why she would save one old shoe if there wasn't a pair. Anyway, there's more. I found this riddle hidden behind the portrait of Mama that my father painted before he left."

"No way! What does it say?"

"It says: It was early in the West
    at the Capitol and 16th Honest Abe
    Silver is the key three times
    for a special little babe."

"Who do you think wrote it?" asked Adam.

"I have no clue, but Gramps says it was inside the silver shoe," said Silvie.

"Now we're getting somewhere!"

"Yeah, where are we getting?"

"I don't know, but it was in the shoe. That's gotta mean something, Blake!"

"Yeah, Westin, I just wish I could figure out what."

"Any ideas?"

"I'm not totally sure, but, here goes;" Silvie replied. "Honest Abe was a nickname for the sixteenth President of the United States, Abraham Lincoln, and there was a portrait of Lincoln at the Capitol."

Silvie reached into her jeans pocket and pulled out the elevator key. "Gramps told me my father worked at the Capitol. Maybe he knew something about the underground tunnels. Maybe he worked there when the first portrait of the sixteenth president, Honest Abe Lincoln, was stolen. Maybe he saw someone use a key like the one we found to go into the elevator, and he got a key and used it to get the painting out of the Capitol. Maybe that's why Revi said the key and my father have something to do with the first stolen painting of Lincoln," said Silvie.

"That's it?" asked Adam.

"Yeah, or maybe my father is the one who took the first portrait of Lincoln from the Capitol."

"Wow, that's a trip. But it doesn't explain the Silver Heels part or the hidden treasure part."

"The only thing I can figure is that Silver Heels lived early in the west. I do know my father was looking for a treasure. Why is it that guys always think there's a treasure somewhere?"

"Because maybe there is, and if there is, you could find it. Can't you see anything else in the riddle? You're the queen of solving puzzles, Silvie Blake!"

"Well if I am, I'm not seeing anything else here, Adam Samuel Westin the Sixth!" said Silvie, in frustration.

"You just sounded like Crabtree! You don't have to use my whole name like that! Come on, Blake, you can do this!"

There was a silent pause on the phone. Silvie stared at the riddle; then, out of habit she started rearranging letters.

"Wait a second, Westin, I think I'm getting something new," said Silvie.

"What? What are you getting?" Adam asked.

"I don't believe this! Can you meet me at the Capitol tomorrow around nine o'clock?"

"Sure; why?"

"I have an idea."

"Tell me, Blake."

"Actually, Westin, I'd rather show you tomorrow!"

Chapter 30

"Blake! Don't hang up! Tell me now!" pleaded Adam.

"You have to see this with your own eyes to believe it, Westin," said Silvie. "I'll show you tomorrow. Gramps has to go somewhere in the morning so he won't mind that I'm meeting you to work on our project."

"I'll never be able to sleep tonight."

"Look, I could be way off. This will keep until morning."

"Okay, Blake, I'll be there. Bring the riddle and everything else. I want to see it all — the shoe, the locket, and the photo of your great-great grandma, Josie."

"I will. See you in the morning... and Adam..."

"Yeah?" he said.

"Thanks for your help," said Silvie.

After she hung up, Silvie grabbed her purple backpack from the closet. She put in the silver-heeled shoe, the half locket, and the photo of Gram with Great-Great Grandma Josie. She looked at the riddle and her own handwritten notes one more time. Then she added them to the contents in the backpack.

Silvie got ready for bed. When she took off her jeans the elevator key fell out. She picked it up and set it on top of her dresser. She put on her pajamas. Gramps knocked and poked his head into her room.

"Good night, Gramps," Silvie said. She hugged him and kissed his scratchy cheek.

Gramps looked at Silvie. There was something in his eyes that she couldn't read. He kissed her and said, "Sleep tight."

Silvie called Millie. The cat came running and she picked Millie up. She turned off the lamp on her nightstand and crawled into bed with her kitty.

Silvie didn't think she would be able to sleep, so much had happened today. She heard Gramps brush his teeth and blow his nose loudly a few times. Then, the house got quiet. She smoothed the hair on top of Millie's head between her ears. The cat purred so loudly; it sounded like a motor on Silvie's chest. Silvie ran the words from the riddle through her mind until she dozed off.

Before Silvie knew it, she opened her eyes and saw the Friday morning sun peeking through her curtains. She couldn't believe she had been able to sleep, but she must have drifted off during the night. It was the first day of spring break. She got out of bed, pulled on her robe, and stepped into her slippers. It was too cold to run around on the hardwood floors barefoot.

She smelled coffee brewing as she bounced downstairs.

"Good morning!" called Gramps. "How about some bacon and scrambled eggs?"

"That sounds great. Do we have strawberry jam for toast?" asked Silvie.

"You bet! I'll cook the bacon and eggs. You're on toast duty."

Silvie fed Millie, and then popped two slices of bread into the toaster.

"What are you doing today?" asked Gramps.

"I'm meeting Adam back at the Capitol," said Silvie.

"Are you going to tour it again?"

"Not really. There are a few things I want to see."

"I have an appointment at nine o'clock this morning. Maybe, I can treat you and your friend Adam to lunch."

"Can we go to the McDonald's on Colfax across from the Capitol?"

"Sure, I'll meet you there at eleven forty-five. That way we'll be ahead of the lunch rush."

Gramps patted the extra grease off the bacon and put two slices on Silvie's plate, followed by a pile of scrambled eggs. She buttered toast for both of them and then slathered her piece with strawberry jam. They ate as if they were loading up for a day of hard labor out on the farm.

"Breakfast is the most important meal of day," said Gramps.

"I know, Gramps, I think we're doing a good job on it here," said Silvie.

They both laughed. After the dishes were washed, Silvie went back upstairs and brushed her teeth. She combed the pillow shapes out of her hair. She looked at her scarred face. She had actually forgotten about it for a while last night, but here it was staring at her in the mirror.

Silvie finished getting ready. She dropped the silver key into her pocket. She didn't plan to ride the elevator or go into the tunnel again today, but she wanted to be prepared.

"I can give you a ride to the Capitol," called Gramps from his bedroom.

"If I go now, I'll be too early," said Silvie. "I can catch the eight-forty bus." She watched Gramps put on his jacket and hat, then kissed him goodbye.

"I'll see you at lunch. Be careful," Gramps said.

"I am always careful, Gramps; don't worry," said Silvie.

She turned on the T.V. to fill twenty minutes. Millie jumped onto her lap and Silvie teased her for a bit with a stray piece of string.

"The portrait of Abraham Lincoln has been returned to its rightful spot in the Colorado State Capitol," said the T.V. announcer. "The police followed a phone tip and recovered the stolen painting from a campsite where a number of homeless people were living."

Silvie looked at the T.V. She saw the painting hanging back up on the wall in the Capitol. The scene switched to the place under the viaduct where she and Adam had found the stolen painting. She saw an officer putting homeless people into a police van. Silvie looked down at Millie. When she glanced up she saw a woman from the back being guided into the police van. Then, the scene switched to the announcers. All she had seen was a tattered coat and the back of a hat, but Silvie was sure she knew the woman.

Chapter 31

Silvie moved closer to the television. A chill ran up her backbone. She flipped channels, hoping to get another glance at the homeless woman. She tried NBC, ABC, CBS, and then FOX. They had all moved on to today's weather. She pressed the power button on the remote and the screen went dark.

Silvie felt like she knew the woman more than she recognized her. She couldn't see her face; only the woman's back inside of a baggy, worn coat and her hat-covered head. More weirdness! What else is going to happen she wondered.

Silvie ruffled Millie's fur.

"Watch the house, Mill," said Silvie. She put on her jacket and pulled the straps of her backpack onto her shoulders. She walked through the kitchen and grabbed a dollar's worth of quarters, enough for two rides on the RTD bus. She looked at the portrait of Mama for a long moment on her way out. She shrugged and shook her head in sadness. Sometimes she could feel her mother's presence, but mostly she just wanted her back. She walked out into the day, locking the house behind her.

Silvie breathed in the cool, morning air as she made her way to the bus stop. Even though it was chilly, she could taste spring in her nose and mouth. She was at the bus stop for less than a minute when she saw the large rectangular vehicle approaching. She got on the bus and dropped two quarters into the box next to the driver. She slid into a seat near the front and settled next to the window. She took her backpack off and held it on her lap. She couldn't wait to see Adam's reaction to the contents she carried.

The bus cruised west on Colfax Avenue, stopping in front of the twin-towered Cathedral up the street from the Capitol. Silvie grabbed the straps of her backpack and jumped off. She waited for the green light at the intersection and then crossed the street. She spotted Adam sitting on the east steps where they'd entered the building the day before. He stood and waved when he saw her coming.

"Hey Blake, did you bring the stuff?" Adam asked.

"It's all right here," Silvie replied. She sat down on the steps.

Adam plopped beside her. "Let's see it! I can hardly wait!"

Silvie pulled out the photograph of Josie. "This is Gram's grandma. She's the one who had a sick mother."

Adam looked at the picture and nodded.

Silvie felt in the bottom of her backpack and pulled out the half locket.

"I see the B.B.," said Adam. "Those initials certainly don't stand for Silver Heels."

"You're right. I have no idea what they stand for," said Silvie. She reached in and took out the shoe. "How about this?"

"Wow! That could be Silver Heels' shoe," said Adam.

"I guess so. I just don't know what Gram is doing with one shoe, except....."

"Except what?"

"Except the riddle was inside it, according to Gramps."

Silvie took the yellowed paper out of the backpack's front zipper compartment, unfolded it and handed it to Adam.

Adam read the riddle out loud:

"It was early in the West
at the Capitol and 16th Honest Abe
Silver is the key three times
for a special little babe."

"Now, I see what you mean about the sixteenth President being Lincoln at the Capitol," said Silvie. "I think my father could have helped someone take that first portrait of Lincoln because of this riddle."

"Or he could have taken it himself," said Adam.

"Right. What did he do with it if he took it?"

"Maybe he found the last clue to the treasure and left. He was finally rich!"

"I don't think so."

"Why not?" asked Adam.

"Because I don't think he figured out the clue in the very first line," said Silvie.

"Is that what you want to show me in person?"

"You know how I like word puzzles. Last night I was playing with the first line in the riddle while we were talking on the phone. If you rearrange the letters in the word, 'early,' and use the 'w' from 'was,' you can spell 'lawyer.'"

"Lawyer? What could that have to do with it?" asked Adam.

"Not much really, unless you use the 'as' from 'was' and the rest of the line," said Silvie.

"I still don't see anything."

"Well, how about if I separate the 'a' and the 's' and capitalize them?"

"Like initials?"

"Yep, like initials, and then we use 'in the west.'"

"How?"

"Easy; we put 'in' after 'west.'"

Adam's eyes widened and Silvie heard him gasp, "It spells Westin!"

"Yeah, A. S. Westin," said Silvie.

"Adam Samuel Westin!" said Adam.

"Exactly, and if we put 'the' in front of 'lawyer,' we have 'The lawyer A. S. Westin,'" said Silvie. "Does that sound like anyone you know?"

"Oh my gosh!" exclaimed Adam.

"Since you're Adam Samuel Westin the sixth, it's one of the other Adam S. Westins before you."

"Yeah, there were five before me, all lawyers, too." Adam was quiet for a minute. "I think your dad had the second line of the riddle wrong, Blake."

"You mean the Lincoln part?"

"Exactly. Now I have something to show you. Follow me."

Silvie went with Adam down the steps and out to the street.

"You could tell me where we're going," said Silvie.

"You made me wait overnight to see the first line of the riddle for myself," said Adam. "You only have to wait five minutes to see my interpretation of the riddle's second line."

Silvie followed Adam to the corner of Colfax Avenue and Grant Street. They waited for the green light and then crossed. Adam turned left on the north side of Colfax. Silvie quickened her pace to keep up.

Silvie noticed a man sitting up against the side of one of the buildings. He looked into her eyes. She recognized the homeless beggar that she had given her change to the day before on the way to school.

"Wait, Adam," said Silvie.

She pulled out the contents of her jeans pocket. The man didn't have his sign with him, but Silvie figured he could use her other two quarters more than she could. Gramps was meeting her and Adam for lunch and she could ride home with him.

Silvie felt comfortable talking to the stranger with Adam next to her. "Hello again," said Silvie.

Gram and Mama had a tradition of helping people in need and Silvie intended to follow in their footsteps. She opened her palm to the beggar. There were two quarters, a nickel, four pennies and the silver elevator key.

The man stared at her open hand. Silvie looked down and quickly picked the key out of the coins. She gave the man her change. He nodded a thank you.

"Come on," said Adam.

Silvie stuck the key back in her pocket.

They walked west one block. "We're turning here," said Adam.

Silvie looked up at the name on the green and white street sign. Painted in white block letters was Lincoln Avenue.

Chapter 32

Dwayne Beasley had spent a chilly night alone. Since the police broke up the campsite, there were no fires inside of metal trash cans to keep him warm. He drained the contents from his paper bag wrapped bottle. There was barely a swallow left. Drinking had put a soft blanket over his world. He only cared a little bit when the police took some of the wanderers away. He only cared a little bit more when they took her away. After the last drop, he cared a lot less about the whole thing.

Dwayne didn't want to be an alcoholic, but he inherited it from his mother. She probably didn't want to be one either, but she inherited it from her mother. He thought of his mother now. She had hidden her drinking well, especially when they came for visits to check on the children. So many children came in and out of their house. That was how she supported her own kids, by using the money she got for foster children to feed everyone. That, like the hidden alcoholism, was a family tradition.

Dwayne crossed Colfax and walked one block south to 14th Avenue. There was a fried chicken joint there he liked. He waited until a worker took out the trash, then he untied one of the plastic bags. He found what he was looking for: chicken that had sat under the heat lights too long to serve to paying customers. Dwayne liked it fine, and the price was right. It was a bit over-cooked, but it tasted great! There were some hard biscuits, too.

Dwayne ate his fill and then walked along Grant Street from 14th Avenue back to Colfax. He looked up at the sign. Under the words, Colfax Avenue, was printed 1500. "Why don't they just call it 15th Avenue?" he said out loud to the cars speeding by.

He sat down between two buildings. His full stomach made him feel relaxed, and soon he dozed off. Awhile later he awoke. He felt stiff as he struggled to stand. He peeked out around the brick wall to the front corner of the building. He didn't feel like begging just yet.

Dwayne saw an RTD bus stop near the Cathedral on Colfax. He thought he recognized the girl stepping off the bus. Sure enough, it was the school girl who gave him some change the day before. What is she doing back here? he wondered.

Dwayne watched her walk across the street to the Colorado State Capitol. She waved at someone. It was that same boy from the phone booth. Dwayne watched them while they sat on the steps of the Capitol. Then they got up and started walking back toward Colfax. They crossed the street and headed toward him.

"She won't recognize me," Dwayne said to himself.

He watched the girl until she almost passed him. He looked in her eyes. They were kind; they reminded him of her. She was kind too, before he took her key, before he didn't have the nerve to tell her he lost it, before the police took her away.

The girl reached into her pocket and held something out to him. He looked at her open hand. There were coins and an odd-shaped silver key. The key was like the one he had taken from the woman. She couldn't have found the key I dropped in the tunnel, he thought, but it looks so similar. The girl gave him the coins.

"Come on," said the boy.

Dwayne recognized the protective way the boy wanted to get the girl away from him. He'd felt that way about his younger sister a long time ago. The boy and girl reminded him of his sister, but he didn't want to think about his childhood. He was thinking about that key and the treasure. The boy and the girl had just come from the Capitol. Did they know something about the riddle and the treasure?

Dwayne's head hurt. He shook it to clear his thoughts. There's something familiar about that girl, he thought, and she has a silver key. He waited until he saw the two kids walk to the corner of Lincoln and Colfax Avenues. They paused for a moment. He waited until they turned right and disappeared around the corner; and then he got up and followed them.

Chapter 33

Silvie turned with Adam around the corner at Colfax and Lincoln Avenues.

"I've never been down this street before," she said.

"This is Lincoln. The two streets east are Sherman and Grant. I guess they had a Civil War theme going when they named them," said Adam.

"I'm sure you won't tell me where we're going," said Silvie.

"You're right!" said Adam. "You'll know in another half a block."

Silvie kept up with his steady strides. The block was lined with various Victorian and Denver Square styled houses. As they neared the corner of 16th and Lincoln the houses turned to mansions.

"We're going there," said Adam, pointing to the end of the block.

Silvie saw a stately mansion with a huge round porch. There were large, ornate windows on each of the three floors.

They stopped on the sidewalk at the bottom of the curved concrete steps ascending to the porch. A wooden sign in the yard with brass numbers and letters on it read:

Law Offices of Westin, Westin, & Westin

1600 Lincoln Avenue

"Is this your dad's office with the red roof we saw from the Capitol dome yesterday?" Silvie asked

"This is it," said Adam.

"It's the lawyer A. S. Westin."

"Uh-huh, and it's at 16th and Honest Abe also known as 16th and Lincoln Avenue."

"How long has this law office been here?"

"Since my great-great-great grandfather started practicing law in the 1800s."

"I see," said Silvie, letting the information settle in her brain.

"Let's go in," said Adam. "You can meet my dad and grandfather. My great-granddaddy comes in every morning and works until lunch time. He's probably here, too."

"Wow! It's really set up in your family for you to be a lawyer," said Silvie.

"Don't remind me," said Adam.

Silvie followed him up the curved steps. Adam turned the ornate brass knob on the leaded glass and carved wooden door. "After you," he said.

The light in the entryway was yellow and warm. A gray-haired woman wearing an earpiece sat behind a large cherry wood desk. She looked up at Silvie, raising her index finger as a signal to wait a moment.

"Good morning. Westin, Westin, and Westin," the woman said into the microphone attached to an earpiece. "May I help you?"

Adam waved at the receptionist. She smiled brightly at him.

"I'll fax that right away. Good-bye," said the receptionist. She stood up and said, "Adam! It's so nice of you to visit us on the first day of your spring break."

"Hi Marie. Is my dad in?" asked Adam.

"He's in court this morning. Can your grandfather help you?" asked Marie.

"We'll find out," said Adam.

"Who's your friend?" She gestured toward Silvie.

"This is Silvie Blake. She's in my class at school. Silvie, meet Marie. She keeps everyone in my family organized."

"It's nice to meet you," said Marie.

Silvie stepped forward and shook Marie's hand. Mama had taught her to look into people's eyes and shake their hand firmly when she was being introduced. The act sent a pang of sadness into Silvie's heart.

Marie pushed some buttons on a mini switchboard. "Mr. Westin, your grandson and his friend are here to see you."

After a pause, she said, "I'll send them in."

Silvie followed Adam down a long hall and into a large room with a three-paned, bay window. The walls were lined with dark, wooden shelves. She had never seen so many books anywhere outside of a library.

The man sitting behind a large, oak desk in the middle of the room had soft, blue eyes and brown hair like Adam's with gray at the temples. It was like looking at Adam fifty years from now.

"Hello, Adam," the man said, glancing up from his papers. "We always like to see you at the office. Who is your friend?"

"Hi, Grandfather. This is Silvie Blake from school."

"Hello, Silvie. Are you thinking of going into law when you grow up?" he asked.

Silvie heard Adam groan.

"Hello, Mr. Westin. I'm not sure what I'll be when I grow up, but I might consider law. Adam sure talks about it a lot," Silvie said, truthfully.

Adam's grandfather looked at his grandson with visible pride. "We have high hopes for our young Adam," he said.

Silvie could see the conflict in Adam's eyes. She wondered how it would resolve in the future.

"We have a question for you, Grandfather," said Adam, looking relieved to move the conversation forward.

"What is it, son?"

"Silvie found a riddle. We think it leads here," said Adam.

"Really?" said Grandfather Westin. "Let's have a look."

Silvie took the old strip of paper out of her backpack and handed it to Adam's grandfather.

"It certainly looks like it's been around awhile," he said. He read silently. "It's interesting. Why do you think it leads here?"

"Because the Capitol is at the end of this street, and our family law firm is at 16th and Lincoln Avenue," replied Adam.

"You're referring to the second line," said Grandfather Westin.

"If you rearrange the letters in the first line it says, 'the lawyer A. S. Westin,'" added Silvie.

"Ah yes, I see," said Grandfather Westin. "May I ask where you got this, Silvie?"

"It was in a box of old stuff that belonged to my grandmother," said

Silvie.

"I wonder where she got it," said Grandfather Westin.

"Gramps says it was in some stuff Gram's grandmother gave her. Actually, he said it was stuck inside of this," said Silvie. She reached inside her backpack and pulled out the single silver-heeled shoe.

"So, what do you think Grandfather? Why does a riddle from inside an old shoe that belongs to Silvie's family lead here?" asked Adam.

"I'm not sure yet. Let's go upstairs. I want your great-granddaddy to take a look at this, too," said Grandfather Westin.

Silvie followed Adam and his grandfather out of the office. Marie smiled at Silvie when they passed by. They walked up a wooden staircase with thick, oak posts at the bottom. Ornately carved, smaller oak posts ran up from the stairs, each connecting at the top to a smooth, oak banister. It was like a version of the hardwood stairs in Silvie's own house except these were fit for royalty.

"Great-Granddaddy's office is at the top of the stairs," explained Adam. "He likes to watch the neighborhood from up there."

"I can't wait to meet him. You're lucky to have so much of your family here," said Silvie.

"I guess you're right," said Adam. "I never thought about it."

They arrived on an open landing where gold-framed pictures lined the walls. Over an antique bench hung paintings of all the Adam Samuel Westins before Adam.

"I call it the Lawyer Line-up," said Adam.

"Hopefully, we will see your picture on this wall someday, son," said Grandfather Westin.

Adam shrugged.

"Maybe, you can do space law or defend airlines or something like that," suggested Silvie quietly.

"Right, Blake," said Adam.

Grandfather Westin knocked softly on an oak door. He opened it and said, "Do you have a minute, Pop?"

"Come in, and bring Adam and his friend, too," said the man inside.

They entered a large office that had a smaller tri-paned bay window facing onto Lincoln Avenue.

"Great-Granddaddy, this is my friend, Silvie Blake, from school," said Adam.

Silvie recognized the white-haired man who had watched her class get off the bus yesterday at the Capitol. She now figured he must have been looking for Adam in the crowd of kids.

"Hello, Mr. Westin. I'm pleased to meet you," Silvie said, shaking his hand.

The elder Westin nodded at her. "I'm pleased to meet you, Miss Blake, is it?"

"Yes, Sir," said Silvie, feeling an immediate respect for Adam's great-grandfather.

"What brings all of you young people up here to see me?" he asked.

Grandfather Westin handed the slip of paper to his father. "Silvie found this riddle, and she and Adam followed the clues to our office," said Grandfather Westin.

"I see. Where did you find this paper, young lady?" asked Great-Granddaddy.

"It was actually hidden behind a portrait of my mother that my father painted, but Gramps told me it originally came from inside this old shoe," replied Silvie.

"And where did your Gramps get that old shoe?" he asked.

Silvie told him about Gram's box and pulled the other items out of her backpack. "I guess Gram kept this old shoe because that's where she found the riddle."

Great-Granddaddy studied the picture of Josie and Gram for a moment.

"It's good, she kept it," he said. He bent down in his chair and opened a drawer in his massive desk. Silvie heard shuffling as he searched for something.

"Let's see now," he said.

He lifted a rectangular shape wrapped in brown paper out of the drawer.

He slowly unwrapped the object. Silvie could see that it was a shoe and it had a silver heel on it.

Great-Granddaddy placed the shoe on his desk next to the one Silvie had brought. "Well, I'll be," he said. "They match."

Chapter 34

"Yes, they do match," said Silvie, hardly believing her eyes. "I feel like I'm in a scene out of Cinderella."

"We don't have a prince here at the law office to whisk you away," said Great-Granddaddy chuckling, "but I think we do have something that can change your life for the better."

Silvie looked at Adam. He shrugged.

"What do you mean, Mr. Westin?" asked Silvie.

"You say this is a photograph of your great-great grandmother, Josie. Do you have any proof that she is related to you?"

"Only a letter I found behind Gram's photograph. It was written to Gram on her wedding day, and it was signed by her grandmother, Josie. Someone even called me Josie yesterday," explained Silvie.

"Who was that?" asked Adam's grandfather.

"It was a worker at the state Capitol. I think she might have known Gram or her mother," said Silvie.

"That's interesting. You may want to go back and talk with her some more," said Grandfather Westin.

"Yes, I think I do," said Silvie. "After I found the letter behind Gram's picture, I found this photograph of her with her grandmother, Josie, in the box with the rest of the stuff."

"Well, Silvie Blake, I believe we've been waiting for one of the women in your family to arrive for a long time," said Great-Granddaddy.

"Why is that, Sir?" she asked.

He nodded to his son. Adam's grandfather crossed the room. He grabbed the edge of a mountain scene painting hanging on the wall. He swung it open sideways to reveal a wall safe.

"Wow! I didn't know that was there!" exclaimed Adam.

Grandfather Westin punched in some numbers on a computer pad. A metal door opened. He pulled out a wooden box and placed it on the desk, then closed the safe and put the painting back in place.

"Open it, Silvie," he said.

She lifted the wooden lid. Inside there was a solid gold bar, half of a silver locket with the initials S. H., a strip of paper with a copy of the riddle on it, and a folded piece of yellowed paper.

"You have a copy of the riddle, too?" said Silvie.

"Yes, go ahead and read the other paper," said Great-Granddaddy.

Silvie took the paper out of the box and unfolded it. She read:

"Dear Mr. Adam S. Westin, Attorney at Law,

Thank you for agreeing to find a family to care for my daughter, Josie. I am sending all of the gold given to me by Josie's father. I hope it will cover her care and even support her into adulthood. I'm including my silver heeled dancing shoes. She can remember me by them. I will never wear them again. Please take as much of the gold as you need to pay for your services.

Thank you,

Silver Heels"

"My grandfather was the first Adam Samuel Westin," said Great-Granddaddy. "He's the one this letter was written to. He told me the story many times of how he met Silver Heels on one of his trips when he passed through a town called Buckskin Joe. Sometime later, Silver Heels got sick, and a woman who cared for her named Aunt Martha arrived with a package containing some gold, a pair of silver heeled dancing shoes, and a little girl named

Josie."

"So Josie's mother was Silver Heels?" asked Silvie, softly.

"That's right, Silvie," replied Great-Granddaddy. "My grandfather put most of the gold in a trust and found a family by the name of Beasley to raise the child. He sent them enough money each month for her. One day Aunt Martha came back to our office. She gave my grandfather the locket with the initials B. B. on one side and S. H. on the other. She said that Silver Heels was gone."

"It's the other half of the locket from Gram's box," said Silvie. B.B. must stand for Bill Buck.

"You're right. My grandfather sent half of the locket and one of Silver Heels' shoes with the riddle in it to Josie at the Beasley house. She was a teenager by then. For some time, he had suspected her foster mother, Mrs. Beasley, was an alcoholic. My grandfather didn't want to trust her with information about Josie's inheritance, so he gave Josie clues to piece together her background. My grandfather liked riddles and puzzles. He used a riddle hoping Josie would figure it out and come to the law firm on her own."

"Did she ever come?" asked Silvie.

"No, she took off and left no word of her whereabouts. At least, now we know she took the half locket, shoe, and riddle with her. Maybe, she didn't want her foster mother to claim part of her fortune. Maybe, she planned to come see us when she got older. Maybe, she thought it was all a joke."

"Didn't your grandfather ever try to find her?" asked Adam.

"You bet he did. He even asked his son, my father, who was grown and a lawyer by then, to go and look for Josie. They both tried, but they couldn't find her. My grandfather and father felt terrible. They invested the gold, and its value has since grown. They searched for Josie and her family for a long time. I searched, my son here searched, and Adam's father has searched. We have hoped and wished that we would find one of Silver Heels' descendants. We have had no luck until now. It looks like our youngest Westin has accomplished what none of us have been able to before now. Adam brought you here, Silvie."

"Wow, Blake, it looks like you're the great-great-great granddaughter of Silver Heels," said Adam. "Maybe that's why you always wanted to be a dancer."

Silvie drew in a deep breath. "I can hardly believe it. Mama or Gram never mentioned anything about this."

"I'm sure they didn't know," said Grandfather Westin. "The Beasleys probably never told Josie she could find out about her mother at the Westin law firm. I'm surprised the shoe with the riddle ever made it into your grandmother's box of keepsakes."

"I'm also certain your mama and grandmother didn't know," said Great-Granddaddy. "But now you know who you are, Silvie, and you're about to find out what else that means."

Chapter 35

"What else could it possibly mean?" asked Silvie.

"It means that you are the owner of some gold that has been invested and grown over time into two million dollars," said Great-Granddaddy.

"Awesome! There's your treasure, Blake!" said Adam. "Your father had a feeling it was there, and he was right!"

Silvie sat down into one of the large leather chairs facing the desk.

"I can't believe it!" she said. "I guess Silver Heels, a silver heeled shoe, and a silver locket are definitely the key three times for a special little babe like the riddle says. It's too bad that Josie never knew she was the special little babe in the last line."

"We need to contact your parents," said Grandfather Westin.

"I live with Gramps," said Silvie.

"Where are your folks?" asked Grandfather Westin.

"My father left before I was born, and my mother volunteered to help with the wounded in Iraq. There was an explosion. The U. S. Government let us know Mama was lost," said Silvie.

She could see pain hit Adam's grandfather and great-grandfather.

"That's tragic!" said Great-Granddaddy.

"We're sorry to hear that, Silvie," said Grandfather Westin. "We'll call your Gramps then."

"We can do better than that. He's meeting Adam and me at the McDonald's on Colfax for lunch at eleven forty-five. Why don't we all go there?" suggested Silvie.

"It's almost eleven-thirty now. By the time we get on our coats and walk down there it will be eleven forty-five," said Grandfather Westin.

"The exercise will be good for me," said Great-Granddaddy, getting up. He reached over to the standing brass coat rack for his hat and coat.

They all walked downstairs. "We'll be back after awhile, Marie," called Grandfather Westin.

Dwayne Beasley saw them coming and walked ahead toward Colfax. The kids had two men with them. What would a couple of kids want with lawyers, he wondered. Did they show the men the key? Was the treasure hidden at the law firm? He picked up his pace, crossed Colfax at the corner, and walked along the street on the opposite side. He could see them approaching the intersection. They turned left and walked east two blocks. He watched them go into the McDonald's. Was the treasure hidden in this hamburger joint across from the Colorado State Capitol?

Dwayne crossed back to the other side of the street. He could beg while he watched them from one of the windows facing Colfax without them ever knowing he was there. If they came out with a package he could run into them and grab it.

"That treasure's mine. I had the key first!" said Dwayne to himself.

Silvie walked with Adam and his grandfathers into the restaurant.

"Here we are," said Grandfather Westin. "Do you see your grandpa?"

Silvie scanned the growing crowd in the hamburger joint. She spotted Gramps sitting at a table across the room facing the door. He waved wildly when their eyes met.

"There he is," said Silvie.

"Who's with him?" asked Adam.

Silvie saw the woman at the same time Adam asked his question. Her back was to them. Silvie saw her from behind, the shape of her shoulders, the back of her head and the color of her hair. She knew instantly it was the woman she had seen on the news that morning.

Chapter 36

Silvie wanted to run to the table. She tried, but everything was moving in slow motion.

Gramps jumped up and motioned toward her. His smile was as big as his whole face. "Silvie!" he called.

Silvie wasn't breathing. Time stopped as she approached the table. The woman turned slowly and faced Silvie. She looked tired, like twenty years had passed instead of one.

"Mama," said Silvie in a hoarse whisper.

Tears filled the woman's eyes and spilled onto her cheeks. Her lips trembled. "I remember now," she said. She stood up and held her arms open to Silvie.

Silvie hugged her gently at first and then hard like she would never let go. "Mama!" she cried from the depths of her soul.

Gramps put his arms around the two of them and cried in gruff sobs. After a bit, they moved apart to look at each other.

"Where have you been, Mama?" asked Silvie,

"I don't know. Gramps says I was living on the streets. I remember working in Iraq. I saw such terrible things. There were bombings every day. One night, there was an explosion. I remember running. Maybe, I was hit in the head. I don't know. I don't know how I got back here. I didn't know who I was until Gramps came to get me at the police station. He called my name. When I heard him say Lizzie, I knew it was me."

"She asked for you right away, Silvie. I had to get her out of there. I promised I would take her to you," said Gramps.

"How did you know she was there?" asked Silvie.

"I saw the news report where the police were rounding up homeless people in connection with that stolen painting from the Capitol," explained Gramps. "I saw a woman from the back being put into a police van. I thought maybe it was your mama. I was afraid to hope, but I had to find out for sure. I called the police station last night. They said I could come down and identify her this morning. That's where I had to be at nine o'clock. I didn't want to tell you in case I was wrong."

Silvie couldn't let go of her mother, nor could Mama let go of her. Silvie turned to the Westins. Great-Granddaddy was blowing his nose in a real, cloth hanky. Grandfather Westin and Adam were wiping their eyes.

"This is my family," said Silvie. "Gramps, Mama, this is my friend, Adam, his grandfather and great-granddaddy."

Gramps shook hands with the men.

"So, this is Adam from school. I'm glad to know you!" said Gramps.

"I'm glad to know you too, Mr. Blake," said Adam.

"Can I buy you all lunch?" asked Gramps. "We're celebrating. My daughter has come home!"

"How about if we buy lunch for our clients here?" said Grandfather Westin.

"Clients?" asked Gramps.

"They're lawyers," said Silvie.

They all sat down around the table.

"How did we get to be their clients?" asked Gramps.

"Great-great-great Grandma hired them a long time ago," explained Silvie. I followed the riddle to their office."

"You figured out that old riddle?" asked Gramps.

"The riddle from the shoe?" asked Mama. "I remember that riddle."

"Who's this great-great-great grandma?" asked Gramps.

"Her name was Silver Heels," said Great-Granddaddy, "She was a hero, and she left a bit of money for your daughter and granddaughter."

"Silver Heels? I think I read a legend about her once," said Gramps. "She was a dancer or something, and she took care of miners who were striken with smallpox until they died. They named a mountain after her. It's amazing to know that Gram was related to her. Then again, it's not so far off. It kind of makes sense."

"You say there's a treasure? Silvie's father thought so," said Mama, shaking her head. "He looked, but he never found it. I remember that part, too."

"He didn't know how to look in the right place, but your daughter did," said Great-Granddaddy. "She found it."

"Good work, Silvie!" exclaimed Gramps. "How did you do it?"

"It was all that practice with word puzzles," said Silvie. "If I hadn't ruined my face when I was young, I never would have spent so much time alone working puzzles. I guess it helped me."

"I think your face looks fine," said Grandfather Westin, "but if it bothers you there are laser treatments that will erase most of your scars."

"We don't have money for that," said Silvie.

"Yes, you do, Silvie. Yes, you do," said Grandfather Westin.

"How much money does she have?" asked Gramps.

Grandfather Westin leaned over and whispered into his ear. Silvie saw Gramps' eyes open wide.

"I see!" he said. "What a day this has been!"

"Let's eat lunch," said Great-Granddaddy. "I haven't had one of these hamburgers and fries in years. I'm supposed to watch my cholesterol, but this is a celebration."

Silvie and Adam took orders then left the grownups and went to the counter to pick up lunch.

"Adam, do you think it's weird that our great-great-great grandparents knew each other?" asked Silvie.

"Yeah, it's also weird that we became friends and figured this whole thing out," said Adam.

Dwayne Beasley watched the group from outside the window. There she was, the woman from the homeless campsite. What was she doing with the girl? It looks like some kind of reunion in there, thought Dwayne when he saw them hugging and crying. That proves it! The girl must have something to do with the woman, the key, the riddle and the fortune! A woman handed him a dollar. "Thank you, Ma'am," he grumbled.

The group inside the restaurant finished their lunch. Gramps wrote his address and phone number on a napkin and gave it to Grandfather Westin. They gathered their coats. Silvie looped her arm through Mama's as they walked out toward the street.

Silvie saw the man begging at the corner. Mama paused and looked at him for a moment.

"Hello," said Mama, staring hard at him.

The beggar nodded.

Silvie noticed the man looking them over as if he was searching for something with his eyes.

Mama pulled Silvie close to her instinctively.

"I know you," said Mama. "It's from the police station, isn't it?"

The man jerked slightly.

"I think I remember you being there last night," said Mama.

"No, you're mistaken," he said, turning and bolting away.

"I guess we scared him," said Mama.

Gramps, Silvie, and Mama followed Adam's grandfathers to the corner.

"My car is parked here," said Gramps. "Can I give you gentlemen a lift?"

"No thanks," said Great-Granddaddy. "We're only a few blocks from here. We'll be in touch."

Silvie made sure Mama was comfortable in the front seat. Gramps got in the driver's side. Silvie walked around to the passenger side. Before she got in she looked up at the grand Colorado State Capitol. She saw lights on in all of the windows. On the second floor, there was a single silhouette of a woman holding a polishing cloth. Silvie raised her hand and waved to Revi. The woman touched her heart with one hand and waved her polishing cloth back at Silvie. Then, she disappeared.

Chapter 37

Silvie climbed into the back seat of Gramps' midnight blue station wagon. Her heart was filled to bursting with Mama sitting in the front seat heading for home. Gramps turned around and faced Silvie.

"Your mama will have to spend nights at the hospital for a while," he said quietly, though Silvie knew that Mama could hear him.

"Why?" asked Silvie.

"She needs to be under a psychiatrist's care to help with her memory and to help her heal from Post Traumatic Stress Disorder; they call it PTSD for short," explained Gramps. "The doctors told me that she'll likely have bad dreams for some time. Whatever your mama saw and whatever she went through was horrible enough to shut down her conscious mind in order to protect her. She is fragile now."

Mama looked at Gramps and then back at Silvie and smiled.

"I understand," said Silvie, reaching over the seat to gently touch Mama's shoulder. "We'll help you Mama, and you'll get well."

Gramps nodded. He turned around and started the car. Silvie sat back and fastened her seat belt. They drove down Lincoln Avenue so Silvie could point out the Westin law office. Adam and his grandfathers were walking up the curved sidewalk when the Blakes drove past. They waved to one another.

"I'm thinking, now that you and your mama have some money, you'll have enough for college and those ballet lessons you've always wanted," said Gramps.

"And I can pay for laser treatments to get rid of my scars like Grandfather Westin talked about," said Silvie.

"You can if you want to," Gramps replied. "It's as if everything in our lives fell into place today. It's almost as if an angel is watching over us. It's as if Gram is still hanging around."

"It's true," agreed Silvie. "Maybe, Gram and all of my grandmothers are helping us."

Gramps turned on the radio. As they drove the rest of the way home, Silvie couldn't keep her eyes off the back of Mama's head. Even though Mama was here now, Silvie would have to give her up every night for a while.

Gramps parked the car on the street in front of their house. Silvie and Gramps helped Mama walk up the sidewalk and steps onto the porch. Gramps fumbled with the key until the door swung open. Mama stared into the house.

"It's okay Mama; you're home now," said Silvie.

She guided Mama into the house. Mama looked at each item in the entry-way as if she were seeing it for the first time. Her eyes stopped on the portrait of herself.

"Your father painted that. I remember," said Mama.

"Gramps told me," said Silvie.

"Your father had so many secrets. He was always hiding things," said Mama.

It was odd for Silvie to hear Mama talk about her father. Mama hardly mentioned him in the past. It was as if Mama's memory was being activated.

"He left me three things," said Mama. "The most important thing he left me was you, Silvie." Mama put her arm around her daughter. "And he left me this huge painting and a little silver key for good luck. I took it with me to Iraq. Maybe, it was lucky. Maybe, that's why I survived."

He left you a silver key? That's an odd, good luck charm, thought Silvie.

"Where is your good luck key, Mama?"

Mama felt her neck. She pulled a chain out from under her ragged sweater. There was nothing on the chain.

"I guess I lost it," said Mama in a faraway voice.

Silvie nodded. She absentmindedly stuck her hands into her pockets. Her fingers grazed a hard object in her right pocket. She pulled out the silver elevator key.

"That's it! You have it! Was it with my things at the police station?" asked Mama.

Silvie didn't want to confuse Mama or make her feel bad. She thought about what to say and then decided to try the truth.

"It wasn't at the police station, Mama. I found it," said Silvie. Her mind started working like gears inside of a clock, turning on each other with possibilities around and around in her mind. "Maybe, I walked by the spot where you lost it."

Silvie looked into Mama's eyes trying to decide if Mama could have used the elevator key to go into the Capitol and take the Lincoln painting. The police did find the stolen painting at the same campsite where they found Mama. Silvie decided that Mama could not have been in her right mind if she was the one who did it.

"You take the key," said Silvie. "It's yours."

"Put it up on top of my portrait, Silvie. I don't want to wear it around my neck anymore. The key can stay with your father's painting. They can tell each other secrets for eternity."

Silvie got a chair and dragged it over to the painting. She stood on the chair to place the key on top of the portrait. There was plenty of room up there because of the thickness of the canvas. She remembered being surprised by its weight the night before. She climbed down and put the chair away.

"Do you know what I'd like right now?" asked Mama.

"What?" said Silvie.

"I'd like you to come upstairs and help me wash my hair."

"Sure, Mama."

"And I want a bath and clean clothes. We can throw every stitch I have on in the trash can. I want to wear my own clothes."

"The trash can's ready when you are," said Gramps coming into the room.

"Come on Mama, I'll help you," said Silvie.

Silvie took Mama upstairs and helped her wash off the months she must have spent living on the street. She figured if those clothes could talk they would tell a few stories.

Silvie threw away Mama's rags. Afterward, the family sat together in the living room. Silvie told Mama about school and her new friend, Adam. Millie jumped into Mama's lap and purred loudly.

"She's welcoming you home," said Silvie.

"Did we have a cat?" asked Mama, giving Millie a good rubbing all over.

"Gramps let me get her after you left so I wouldn't be so lonely."

"That was a great idea for you and for this cat."

After they finished dinner, Gramps said, "I promised to get you back to the hospital by seven; we'd better go." He whispered to Silvie, "Do you want to come along?"

Tears burned Silvie's eyes. She shook her head and whispered back, "I'd rather be there tomorrow to pick Mama up and bring her home for the day. It will make me too sad to leave her in a hospital tonight."

Gramps nodded, "I understand."

Silvie hugged her mother hard.

"Have sweet dreams tonight," said Mama, kissing Silvie.

Mama had a vacant look in her eyes. Silvie knew that it would take time for her to get better, to fully come home to her family. Silvie hoped that Mama's eyes would fill up with the present, that it would replace whatever past horrors she had seen.

Silvie cried as she watched Gramps help Mama get into the car. She was happy that Mama was alive and had come home, yet sad that she wasn't well.

She walked through the entryway to go upstairs. As she stared at the portrait of Mama, Revi's words popped into her head. "Revi said my father knows what happened to the first stolen portrait of Lincoln from 1994," she said softly. "My father gave Mama the key to the elevator at the Capitol. My father painted this big heavy portrait of Mama."

Silvie suddenly had an idea. It was a long shot, but other amazing things had happened today. She took the painting off the wall and carefully set it on the floor. She removed the silver key from the top and put it back in her pocket.

"Mama said that my father had a lot of secrets," she said out loud. "She said he was always hiding things. Why would he take the time to hang a portrait before he ran off?"

Silvie turned the portrait over to the backside. She got a hammer out of the kitchen drawer and carefully pulled the nails out of the leather strips holding the corners of the frame together. She turned the painting front side up and gently shook it. Something started to wiggle. She shook it a little harder. A canvas broke loose and fell out the back onto the floor. She stared at the painting on the canvas that had been hidden behind Mama's portrait for over ten years. Staring back at her was the face of Abraham Lincoln.

Chapter 38

A few blocks from the hamburger joint and the Capitol, Dwayne Beasley caught his breath. She recognizes me, Dwayne thought to himself. Soon, she will remember why.

She had been taken by the police and now she was meeting with lawyers from that Westin law firm. That was all Dwayne needed to know.

"It won't take her long to figure out that I took her key," Dwayne said to himself. "She'll know I stole the Lincoln portrait from the Capitol and she'll tell them it was me. Those lawyers will get it out of her if the police don't. At least I don't have much to pack." He laughed out loud at his own joke. "I don't have anything to pack. I made a few bucks begging here at this corner. My thumb and a little luck is all I need right now."

Dwayne Beasley's luck came by within ten minutes. A red pick-up pulled over.

"Where are you headed?" asked the driver as Dwayne ran up to the passenger side.

"I'm heading for California. I've had enough cold weather," Dwayne replied.

The driver laughed. "I'm not going that far, but I can get you to Utah. You'll have to catch another ride from there."

"No problem," said Dwayne. "I appreciate you taking me as far as you can. I figure it'll take quite a few rides to get to California, but I've got plenty of time."

Dwayne wasn't leaving much behind. He thought of his younger sister who had left the family long ago. She found him once. She said she had become a teacher and changed her last name to Crabtree. She said he could remember her name if he thought about the crabapple tree in their backyard, the one they used to play under with all of the other children that came and went. She said it would help him remember in case he ever wanted to find her.

Dwayne didn't want to find her. She could be working as a teacher anywhere. Where would he start looking for a Ms. Crabtree? He had no use for family, no use for memories, no use for the past.

Dwayne opened the door to the truck and jumped in. He was done with Denver, done with stolen paintings, and done with the woman from the campsite. He just hoped she was done with him, too!

Chapter 39

Silvie picked up the portrait of Abraham Lincoln. It was signed in red by Lawrence Williams. She knew that she was holding the original Lincoln painting stolen from the Colorado State Capitol in 1994. She was sure that neither Gramps nor Mama had any idea that this painting was hidden behind Mama's portrait. She had to return the painting to the Capitol, and she had to protect her family.

She picked up the phone to call Adam, but hung up before she dialed his number. Her instincts told her she would have to handle this part all by herself. Gramps would be home soon.

Silvie nailed the leather strips back into place and rehung Mama's portrait in its spot. She found some brown paper grocery sacks and string in the storage cabinets on the back porch. She cut the bags open so they lay flat. Then she wrapped the Lincoln painting, taped the edges, and tied it with the string. She carried the painting up to her room and hid it in her closet. She only needed to keep it out of sight until morning.

Silvie got her notebook out of her backpack. She found the page with the list of women's names in her family. She crossed out "sick mother" and wrote "Great-great-great Grandma Silver Heels."

Silvie was interrupted by the sound of the phone ringing. "Hello," she said into the receiver.

"Hey Blake, it's Adam. How's it going with your mom?"

"Hi, Westin. It's fine. She has to spend nights at the psychiatric ward of the hospital for a while until she can handle the Post Traumatic Stress Disorder, and until she can get all of her memory back; but she can come home during the day."

"I'm really glad she's alive, and you got her back home," said Adam.

"Yeah, me too," said Silvie.

"Hey Blake, you really did find a treasure. Your great-great-great grandma left you a fortune! What are you going to do with it?" asked Adam.

"I've been thinking about that. Of course, Gramps and Mama can take whatever they need. I might look into that laser surgery your grandfather talked about, and I'm going to start ballet lessons; and I'll save some for college. After this morning, I'm thinking of law school."

"That all sounds great. I bet there'll be a place for you at the Westin law firm. My grandfathers were both pretty impressed with the way you put clues together and figured things out."

"I've thought of something else to do with the money, Westin. I'm going to pay for you to go to space camp this summer. There's a camp through NASA and the Denver Museum of Nature and Science. I heard about it once when Gramps and I were at the museum. If you go, you can see if you like it."

There was silence on the other end of the phone. Then Adam responded, "Wow, Blake. That's the nicest thing a friend has ever done for me."

"It's a thank-you gift," said Silvie.

"Thank you, Blake! Hey, I almost forgot why I called. My parents are letting me invite some kids over for pizza and game night tomorrow since it's Saturday and spring break. Do you want to come?"

Silvie touched her scarred right cheek out of habit and then she said, "You bet! I'll ask Gramps, but I know he'll say it's okay."

"I live at 1056 Washington Street. I'll see you about five."

"I'll be there. Bye, Westin."

As she hung up, Gramps walked into the house.

"It's all going to be okay," said Gramps. "We just need to give your mama some time to heal."

"I know, Gramps," said Silvie. "Adam called while you were out. Can I go to his house tomorrow at five? His parents are letting him have some kids over for pizza and games."

"Sure, you can go. I'm glad you're making friends."

"Me, too."

"I'm going to the store in the morning to get food for three, and I have to get some prescriptions filled for your mama. Do you want to come?"

"No thanks, Gramps. I want to drop off a note at the Westins' law firm. I want them to know how much I appreciate them taking care of Silver Heels' fortune for so long."

"Good idea. We can pick up your Mama at eleven."

"I'll be home in time. I promise."

"Okay. It's been such an exciting day. I don't know if I can sleep, but I'm going to try."

"Me, too. Please get me up by seven if I don't wake up on my own."

"Will do."

"Good night, Gramps. I love you!"

"I love you, too, Silvie."

Silvie got ready for bed and thought about all that had happened in the past two days. Her life felt different and new. She lay in bed and thought that if she hadn't pulled hot potato soup on herself when she was little, she never would have scarred her face. She never would have spent so much time alone. She would have thought about best friends, make-up, and boys like Maggie and Brittney did, instead of learning how to solve puzzles and how to think.

Millie jumped up onto the bed. Silvie stroked her head until she purred. She thought about how her scars helped her to grow, and to find her great-great-great grandmother. She realized even if she could erase the scars on the outside, she could never erase what they had given her on the inside. The scars reminded her of Silver Heels. Somehow they made her feel close to her great-great-great grandma. She decided that she'd leave her scars for now. She thought of seeing Mama today, and hugging her, and feeling safe and warm. Then she drifted off to sleep.

The next morning, Silvie smelled coffee brewing downstairs and woke up before Gramps had to come and get her. Soon Gramps was off to the store, and Silvie was waiting at the bus stop holding a large brown paper package. She waited past her usual bus and took the next one. It was going east, away from school and the Capitol, away from anywhere she would normally be going.

She found a seat in the back of the bus where she could be alone. All those years of knowing how to be unnoticed served her purpose now. She wrote in pen on the top of the wrapped portrait: "Please deliver to the Colorado State Capitol."

Thirty minutes later, Silvie walked to the front of the bus and told the driver that someone had left a package in one of the back seats. Then she got off and watched the bus continue on its easterly route. With the original Lincoln portrait on its way back to where it belonged, Silvie had one more important thing she needed to do.

Chapter 40

Silvie waited for the next westbound bus and got on. She rode it past her neighborhood to Colfax and Lincoln, using the time to write a thank you note to Adam's grandfathers.

She got off the bus and walked to the Westin law firm. She put her note through the mail slot in the heavy wooden door. They would find it on Monday. She made her way back toward Colfax, crossed the street and headed up the walkway to the Capitol.

"Let me know if you have any questions," said the man at the information desk.

"Okay, thanks," said Silvie.

On the second floor, Silvie looked for Revi around the brass banisters, but couldn't find her. She went back downstairs to the information desk.

"Excuse me, Mr. Weis," said Silvie, reading his name tag, "could you please tell me when a brass polisher named Revi will be in?"

"Let's see," he said, looking through some papers. "I'm sorry, but we don't have anyone by that name working here. There must be some mistake."

Silvie was stunned. The man behind the desk looked at her expectantly. She felt like she had to say something. "She used to work here. Maybe she got a different job somewhere else."

"We have people come and go all the time," said Mr. Weis with a twinkle in his eye. "Have you seen our Lincoln portrait? It's been returned, you know."

"I heard about it on the news," said Silvie.

"It's wonderful when things get put back the way they are meant to be," said Mr. Weis.

"It sure is," agreed Silvie.

She walked up to the second floor. "Revi, are you still here? Can you hear me?" she asked.

Silvie felt nothing but cool air. She walked up one more floor to glance at the portrait of Lincoln. She wondered if they'd leave this one up or hang the original as soon as it made its way back here.

Silvie bounced down the grand staircase, across the open room, and over to the Women's Gold Tapestry. There was Silver Heels, her great-great-great grandmother.

"Thank you, Revi," Silvie said softly. "You brought Mama home and you brought me to your fortune. Maybe your job is finished here. Maybe you're like the pilots from that crashed plane that Adam talked about. They stopped appearing after they got all the parts back from their plane. Maybe you can rest now."

If Revi was a ghost she seemed very real. If she was a ghost, Silvie was glad she came back to help her and Silvie might rethink her beliefs.

Silvie thought about all that she had found in the last couple of days. I found the first and second stolen Lincoln portraits and solved the Capitol case. I found a missing part of our family tree and Silver Heels, my great-great-great grandmother. I found out the truth about my father and I found Mama. Mostly, I found confidence. I found myself.

Silvie smiled. She touched her heart with one hand and waved at the stitched image of Silver Heels with the other.

She headed out past the information desk.

"I saw the painting. Have a nice day, Mr. Weis," she said.

"You can call me Stan, young lady. Have a nice day yourself," he said.

"Okay, bye Stan," said Silvie.

Silvie walked to the bus stop, thinking about ghosts and whether or not she believed in them. She decided that she might believe in them at this moment because she knew for certain that she believed there were some things that she would never know for sure. She believed that someone named Revi had helped her and that by some miracle Mama had come home. With all she had done in the past two days she believed in herself.

Silvie knew that sometimes things happened, coincidentally. Sometimes they didn't make sense; and sometimes, they fell into place perfectly.

She got on the bus and headed for home. For the first time in a long time, everything felt right. She smiled as she watched her city zip by through the windows. Mr. Weis was right. It was wonderful when things got put back the way they were meant to be. He was so friendly, Silvie thought; he told me to call him Stan. Then she remembered how Revi had told her that names were important and she gasped. She didn't need paper and pencil. She couldn't believe she didn't see it immediately.

I guess Adam's great-great-great grandfather is standing guard until the original stolen painting from 1994 gets back to the Capitol, thought Silvie. He probably feels responsible since his riddle started this whole mess to begin with.

She figured by the time she could call Adam and they could get back to the Capitol. Mr. Stan Weis would be gone; his work would be finished.

Silvie couldn't wait to tell Adam that Stan Weis's name unscrambled was A. S. Westin!